TRIBE WARRIOR

TRIBE WARRIOR

Book One
of
The Deer Tribe Saga

By
Caspar Walsh

a Write to Freedom publication

**Front cover artwork, Philip Harris
Back cover artwork and all other artwork,
Alex Fox-Robinson**

ISBN-13: 978-1492326366

PRAISE FOR THE AUTHOR

'**Blood Road**' all books available online in paperback an e book:
"Pitch-perfect. The characterisation - precise, economical and crediting his readers with insight in a carefully structured plot. It is Caspar Walsh's principal achievement that in tackling something so achingly familiar, he makes it feel fresh, challenging and capable of reform"

- The Independent

"An authentic literary voice. Here is an author to watch - and read."
Andrew Taylor - winner of the CWA Cartier Diamond Dagger

'**Criminal**' "This is a fine, unsparing book about what addiction does to all the lives it touches. Caspar Walsh's childhood almost took him down the same path of self-destruction as his charismatic but predatory father. If you want to understand why our prisons are bulging, and where some hope for the future may lie, read this book. Caspar Walsh strips his own life back to the bone as he writes about this child's ferocious love for a father who can't help loving him less than drugs, alcohol, and the fix of crime".

- Helen Dunmore.

"A surprisingly touching, beautifully written tale of the determination of a young lad not to follow in his dad's footsteps. Remarkably, while peppered with hair-raising accounts of scrapes with the cops, violence and abuse, 'Criminal' never loses its sense of optimism and the characters are vividly brought to life"

- News of the World

"I thought it was an extraordinary autobiography. Vibrantly written with one of the most compelling characters in Caspar's father that I've come across in a long time. It's a masterful portrayal of the two sides of a man and demonstrates with absolute clarity how confusing love can be within an abusive relationship."

- Minette Walters

"Thankfully, Walsh's abused, drug crazed, sham glam criminal childhood landed him in prison rather than the morgue. The journey from there to where he is now is redemptive, fuelled by a quiet heroism that is deeply moving."

- Peter Florence - Director of the Hay Literary Festival

Amazon reviews
Criminal. Five star ratings

"I couldn't put this down and finished it in just three days. I'm not ashamed to admit I cried at the end. Read it. This should be on every teenager's reading list."

- D Smith

"This is both a wonderful book and an unflinching act of generosity and courage."

- Nick T

"A deeply impressive book with well-rounded and articulate characters. Highly recommended. Deserves a wide readership."

- Russell Manley

"An Amazon customer said it was one of the best books they had ever read and they were right."

- Faye

Blood Road. 100% Five star rating
Reader reviews:

"Highly recommended, you'll not put it down till you find out how Nick and the kids extricate themselves from a really nasty twisted no hope situation."

- Ben Brangwyn

"Caspar Walsh is a writer to admire and look out for, from his first book Criminal to Blood Road his material is worth reading and sharing...good book club subjects."

- GL Copely-Williams

"A brilliant read that feels very real and authentic. The story grabbed me from the start but it was the last section of the book that I really could not put down."

- NIcki257

"Wow! After the "punch in the gut" prologue, I couldn't put it down; the excellent writing had me on the edge of my seat, and I had absolutely no idea how it would end. I'll say no more...! What a glimpse into another world that I'm sure stems from the author's personal experience. Not for the faint-hearted!"

- Crackerjack

ABOUT THE AUTHOR

Using key elements of his life long study and love of mythology, Tribe Warrior has been drawn from Caspar's extensive work with disaffected youth in and out of prison over the last fifteen years. To date, over three hundred students have experienced Tribe Warrior. The response to the story has been exceptional with students always wanting more. Tribe Warrior continues to mirror Caspar's own extraordinary, redemptive journey through life.

Caspar Walsh is the author of the powerful and moving memoir, Criminal and Blood Road, a semi autobiographical crime novel set in contemporary Britain. Both books were published to international critical acclaim. Caspar writes regular features and comment for The Guardian and Observer and a column for Positive News. He has written two feature-length docu-dramas and several short stories for BBC Radio 4 and regularly broadcasts on local and national radio and television. He is the founder of the award winning youth mentoring charity, Write to Freedom. He currently lives in Devon and is writing his first graphic novel.

ACKNOWLEDGMENTS

I dedicate this book to the power of dreams which is exactly where it came from one dark night in Devon; to the many young men who come from prison and the streets onto the wilds of Dartmoor to share the adventure, you have inspired so much of what is written in these pages. To Lindsay Clarke, Parzifal, C.J. Jung, Robert Johnson, colleagues and collaborators, Robin Bowman, Broo Doherty, Marcel Celtel, Elaine Pope, Toni Keating, all at Ashfield, Michael Boyle, Paul McNicholls, Gavin Blench, Ben Brangwyn, David Berg, Mike Jones, Richenda Macgregor. The many warrior poets within The Mankind Project, Bill Kauth, Steve Kushner, Michael C Jones, the Bristol & Bath and Dartmoor Mission Groups for your many years unflinching support. To the Fellowship. To my father and all fathers, whose invisible knife cuts set us on journeys of fierce adventure, if only we are able to open our eyes and see the magnificent paths they set us on. To the many Serra's who have shown me the way; to Maklan. And finally to Amber, whose pureness of spirit and wildness of heart shows me that the romantic love of the stories of old, is alive and kicking. Thank you, bless you all. I am nowt without you.

Books by Caspar Walsh
Criminal
Blood Road

www.casparwalsh.co.uk

CHAPTER ONE

THE VILLAGE

New Moon Rising

*There is danger here. Danger and death. I can smell it. My legs...
won't work properly. Not now. Don't do this to me... keep moving
Maklan, keep moving... or die.*

*Light's getting bigger, brighter. Must be a village. Never heard
of any villages out this far south, so close to the moor. Must get to
the fire. Food. Must get some food and water, something to drink,
anything. Been in this wood too long, no sleep, no food. Finished.
No energy. Talking to myself like a madman.*

You are a madman.

*Leave me alone. Sick of you. In my head, day and night, on and
on. Just leave me.*

*Only a madman would be out here on his own with nothing
but a dagger to protect him from the wolves and boars.*

Shut... wait. Drums... getting louder. A lot of drums.

Keep going.

*Legs shaking so much. Need to stop them shaking. Can't look
weak. Get it together. Must be because I'm... tired... hungry. That's
it. Hungry.*

That's not hunger. Face it, you're scared.

Leave me.

Keep moving. Just keep moving.

What's that sound?

A war beat; a warning to anyone outside the boundary, to intruders, to me. Must eat. Keep moving. Quiet.

Where in Thunor's name is it coming from?

The fire, over there. Drums round the fire. Lot of drums.

What the... 'Aaahch!!' *Shut up, Maklan! What did I just run into?!*

You walked into a boulder you idiot.

See if there's any blood.

It's bad. Bad wound out here... it's all over.

If there's blood, you need to stop it.

It's deep. Can feel the blood. Not too deep.

Get down. Close to the ground. Stay still.

So hungry... can't see straight.

You need to move. Watch out for boulders, stumps, Deer Tribe-stalking Maklan, foot down... easy on the earth, step-by-step, easy. You remember this. You know how to do this. Keep away from twigs, bracken, branches underfoot, feel for them. Foot down only on what is soft... quiet. Keep low, slow, steady, use your ears, eyes, gut. You can do this.

No trees ahead. Keep moving.

Keep moving. Or die of starvation out here.

What's that?! Stop. There it is again. That sound. Behind me. Don't move. Get down. So dark down here, can't even see the ground. Like looking into the black hole of space... no stars.

There it is again that sound. Moving. Something's moving toward me. What in Thunor's name is it? It's coming at me. Get your blade out... get your bla...

'OOFfff!' *WHAT IS THAT ON MY BACK!?! Something... attacking me! Can't breathe, too close to the ground, can't get up, can't fight it, can't get to my blade. Don't... don't, don't push me, not into the earth. Can't breathe... mud in mouth. Think. THINK, Maklan. Not going to die, not here, not in this dark place. Not my time to fly to the sky gods. Not drowning in this ground.*

I know what's on my back. Know this smell, the breath, from my village. Nasty bitter tang of human sweat and alcohol, heat, aggression. He's strong... heavy. Can't fight back against this... not enough strength... to fight... this. Knocked the air out of me... now trying to finish me, drown me in this mud.

Death coming.

Can feel it. Can't think straight. Thoughts... blacking... not death or sky gods. Not here.

FIGHT, Maklan!

Wait. Gone?! Where? Get up... get up! Move before he comes back.

'GET UP!'

Blade out. Get ready. Where's my blade?!

CHAPTER TWO

TRIBE-BROTHER

Two moons before

Sanfar stands in front of Maklan in the beechwood half-a-day's walk beyond the boundary of their village. The wind is strong in the treetops. It moves around as if it had an angry mind of its own, like it's searching for something to destroy. An explosion of branches and leaves and twigs is scattered across the forest floor from the earlier storm. The wind has calmed but it still rages round. Sanfar sways in rhythm to the movement of the wind. Maklan knows that what moves his blood-brother side to side is not the wind, it is the wine.

'Thunor's sake, Sanfar, you're drunk... again.'

Sanfar sneers at him. 'Swat iff I is?' He looks up into the trees to see the movement of the forest above, grinning like a child seeing a new toy.

'You've changed.' Maklan stares straight at him.

'We've all changed. Thass what growing up's all about, brother. Can't all play with our little wooden toys forever. Some of us have to grow up... you know, moove on.'

The memory of slowly moving hands flashes into Maklan's mind. His real brother, Tenmar's, Sanfar's and his, one knife, three slits, the top of each of their young thumbs. Crimson blood seeps from reed-thin cuts; thumbs are pressed together, the bloods of their fathers, their families, mixed forever. The memory of the words spoken between them that night on the snow-covered high moor, when they each were ten summers old, fall from Maklan's mouth:

'"Till we draw our last breath, till our bodies are cold in the ground... we stick together, brothers, warriors, hunters, friends for life." That's what we said. Now you're going back on that. Breaking your word, your promise.'

'That was a long time ago... everything hazz... changed.' Sanfar slumps down onto his arse, picks up a twig and starts clumsily to strip it of its bark.

'Not for me.' Maklan glares at him. 'I'm still here, we're still blood-brothers. I keep my word. You don't know what you're talking about, you're off your head. You'll become like our fathers and you'll waste your life... just like them.'

'No chance.' Anger rises sharply in Sanfar's voice. 'I know what I'm doing. I have this under control.' He reaches for the leather drinking-gourd, raises it to his lips and swigs. Wine pours down his face and neck, dribbling red like a freshly drawn knife cut. Maklan steps forward to grab it from him. Sanfar steps back and waves his finger at Maklan.

'Now, now. Tut, tut brother. If you want some of this you have to get your own.' He chuckles to himself and continues to drink, draining the wine from its container. He lets his hand drop to his side. He looks about him like a dazed, punch-drunk baby. Half scared, half happy.

'Come on, brother. Come back to the village. You can't do this, not on your own. You can't go. Sleep it off. I'll stay with you. We can talk in the morning. Talk it all through. Go hunting. Chase some storms, get some rabbit. Like old times.'

'Not interested in your little storms and your little rabbits. Thass for babies. Have all I need here.' Sanfar chucks the leather gourd into the bushes.

Maklan looks down at his blood-brother, sadness in his eyes and a pain in his heart. He shakes his head, turns and walks back in the direction of the village. He hears the mumbled singing of a familiar song coming from Sanfar, out of tune, words jumbled, trying to beat back the gentle roar of the wind. Maklan continues to walk, heading out of the wood, back in the direction of the village. The song is lost to the storm. Maklan feels a single tear roll onto his cheek. He wipes it defiantly away. He keeps walking.

Chapter Three

BANISHED

Sanfar watches Maklan walk away. Out of the wood, back onto the moor. He tries to sing to himself to take away the pain of watching his tribe-brother leave him in this cold place. The wind in the trees drowns out the sound of his broken, tearful voice. The leather drinking-gourd lies beside him, empty. He is drunk but it doesn't take away the pain he feels in his heart. He is alone in this place but he prefers that to being back in his village, away from the man who forced him out here, far from his tribe. Sanfar knows he has given Maklan no choice. The images of the seasons spent in his village imprisoned in a pact of silence haunt him daily. These images, these memories will always be with him. The nights he left his family hut, knowing if he did not, the man he went to every new moon would have Sanfar's father thrown out of the village. The man that Sanfar went to, walking through the inky darkness of his sleeping village, had seen Sanfar's father take seed from the grain store, more than his share. Theft from anyone in the village is punished severely. The elders seldom decree anything less than banishment. Sometimes for only a few weeks but being banished always places shame on the family. Shame clings to the guilty like a sticky ghost. The entire family is tarred with the same brush, no matter what the reason for banishing, no matter how difficult the family's life is.

Sanfar's father is not by nature a thief. He took the grain that night because the hunting had been bad all winter. His children and his wife were starving. There was not enough food to go around the village. The man of each household has a responsibility to feed his family. He can get help from the elders but that is limited. There was no more food to feed the starving families. Sanfar's father had taken enough grain to feed his children and his wife but not himself. The man who had seen him enter the grain store that night was a loner; no family, no children and few friends. Few know why they do not like him or trust him and they give him a wide berth. He was accepted in the village because he is a good hunter and he often shares his kill with the children, never the adults. But even he had struggled to find meat this winter. He came to Sanfar one night by the light of the stars. He spoke to him in a whisper, leaning down close to the boy's ear. The words he spoke were soft and kind in tone but in essence full of threat, and filled Sanfar with dread.

'If you don't do what I ask of you, I'll tell the elders of the village what your father did. That he is a thief. There will be great shame on him and your mother, your sister... and you. He will be banished and you may never see him again. You want that? Want your father banished and all that shame on your family for a few handfuls of grain? You want that?'

He told Sanfar what he had to do. That he had to come to his hut by the light of each new moon and do what the lone hunter asked of him. It was done in the hot darkness of the hunter's rotten-smelling hut. For Sanfar, it seemed a small sacrifice to pay to keep his father in the village, in the home. Each new moon, as the night reached its darkest point, he would do what the lone hunter asked. Then, as the village slept soundly, silently make his way back to his family hut. Sanfar kept his shame and his secret from everyone for the first three moons. But it soon became too much to bear, and he went in search of mead to take away the pain and shame. He took his father's summer stock before it was ready. It rotted his gut but it fried his mind and numbed his body enough to block out the memory of what each new moon would bring. But soon his father's new brew store ran dry and Sanfar went in search of more, becoming a shadow thief himself. At first, no one knew where the mead from the village huts was going. No one suspected Sanfar. With each visit to the hunter's hut Sanfar's need for mead increased. His caution around getting caught slackened. Eventually his drunkenness was spotted and he was followed one night as he went on a mead raid to a neighbour's hut. He was dragged before the elders for punishment and was swiftly banished. His father fought angrily and bitterly with the elders to keep his son in the village but they didn't listen. They just repeated the same words, the decision they had come to so quickly.

'He is old enough to hunt. Spring is here and there is enough food for him in the woods, rivers and moors. He will stay away from the village for three moons.'

Sanfar's father wanted to leave with his son but was torn between the need to stay and feed his wife and Sanfar's sister or go with Sanfar and risk his family going hungry again. He chose the lesser of two evils, letting Sanfar go, hoping and praying his son would be able to feed himself. He gave Sanfar his bottle of well-brewed mead and the last of the dried remains of the deer kill and watched his son leave the village. Sanfar didn't look back. His father prayed he would, so he could raise his arm as a sign of his love. Sanfar did not look back.

Sanfar looks for the gourd his father had given him, gives up, comes back and picks up the stripped-down deer bone he and Maklan had eaten from the night before. He looks up, toward the edge of the wood where Maklan's outline disappeared into the tree line.

He sits in that lonely wood for longer than he can remember, losing all track of time. Bitterness and anger rise as the buzz of the mead slowly leaves him. Nightfall creeps like a spider into the wood until he can hardly see his hands in front of him. He won't go back to his village after three moons. If he goes back, there will only be dagger stares and talk and shame. His time in his village is done. He rubs his face with fire-blackened hands, stands up, picks up his pack, turns and heads in the opposite direction to his tribe-brother, south, toward Heartfall.

CHAPTER FOUR

'NO BLOOD DRAWN'

New Moon Rising

Lungs feel like they're burning. But I can breathe again. The air. Breathe. Breathe it in. Think, Maklan. This is no time to die. Not out here. Think.

What in Thunor's name is that?! Not moving. That a tree... or him, the one who just attacked me? Some kind of orange light, not the fire... reflecting, floating there in the dark. Must be seeing things, you're hungry, that's it, just hunger. Father said that could happen if you don't eat enough... you see things.

That's not a vision. That's your blade.

'Too scrawny for the southern clans. Where you crawl out from, rat boy?'

Shadow speaking. Can't see his mouth. Sneering at me, can hear it in his voice. That's no man. A boy... just like me. Big, no more than seventeen summers old I reckon. I'm not afraid of the voice but the size of him scares me. Bigger, stronger.

'I said... where you from and what you doing on our turf, mud-for-brains?'

Run into the darkness, Maklan. Get out of the forest before I run into a tree. No. Don't know this land... don't stand a chance. This land belongs to the shadow in front of me. He'll know it back to front.

Run at him.

Has my blade. Remember why you came here. Sanfar could be here... in this village, a few paces from you now... maybe they know where he is, maybe they've seen him?

'Give you three breaths to speak, then I'll run you through with this pissy little shank, take your guts out first – if you have any.'

Think.

Wait.

Talk to him before he stabs you with your own blade and spills your blood all over the ground. Leaves you here to die in the dark. Boars'll come an' finish you off. Eat you alive.

'My name's Maklan. Deer Tribe of the north.'

'Never 'eard of it. What you want on our land, little man?'

'Food and shelter. Least you can give me for nearly killing me. Been walking two days.'

'Why aren't you with your tribe?'

'I have no tribe.'

Why is he just standing there, saying nothing, looking at me from the dark? Like he's making up his mind, figuring out what to do next?

He's raising his hand. Fingers to his lips, like he's going to whistle. The drums... they've stopped.

'You want food... you do what anyone who steps on our turf does.'

Don't like the sound of this. 'What's that?'

'Get to the village in one piece.'

Do what he wants, get some food and get out of here. 'What? I just head for the fire?'

'You head for the village... you do it blind.'

'I don't get it.'

'You get blindfolded, follow the drumbeat. Main thing is... don't spill a drop of blood, yours or anyone else's. You draw blood, you lose.'

'No one's blindfolding me.'

'You blindfold yourself. You don't, I keep your knife and you walk away, back onto the moor, no food, no shelter. There are wild boar out there, and wolf.'

'If I bleed?'

'Food, no shelter, straight back onto the moor.'

This a trap? Some kind of trick to keep this shadow and his tribe laughing? Belly hollow, tired, so hungry.

Drums started again... different this time. One beat every few seconds...

'Follow the drum, make it to the fire in one piece, no blood, you get food, shelter and your little blade back. Take the blindfold. Put it on.'

You have nothing to lose, Maklan. Do it.

This blindfold stinks of sweat and... blood.

Didn't think it could get any darker. Sounds getting louder. Remember you and Sanfar used to play the blind man. Use your ears... touch. Feel your way forward.

'Remember, rat boy, no blood.'

Need something to guide me. Get a stick. Get on the ground... feel around. Branch. Big one. Break it in two. Snap it over your knee.

Now just wave it round in front of you. Anything in front of me, this hits it first.

Can hear the fire... the drumbeat. Head for it. Head for the drum.

Why my legs shaking?

Because you're scared.

Keep moving.

What is that?!? Swing out, swing out!

Stop!! No blood, remember? That's what the shadow said. Mine or theirs, that's what they meant. Calm yourself, Maklan.

Something out here with me. Not just the shadow. Footsteps on leaves. Moving toward me. More than one.

Remember. No blood.

Keep moving... forward toward the drum... sound of the fire.

Must get some food.

Something's touching me, prodding me, pushing me, shoving me, chucking water, stones, mud at me!

Keep going.

Drumbeat's moving around.

Walked across moor, river, through woodland, to get away from my village, my father, only to get this, blindfolded, mocked.

Something's changing, the air is clearer, like I'm out of the trees... open space. The fire... can feel the heat of the fire.

'Remove the blindfold, Maklan of the Deer Tribe.'

The voice sounds solid, like it's in charge.

Take it off.

That is bright, the fire.

There's a lot of them. Dirty but strong, plenty of weapons, and they look tough. That's him, the tall one, the one that spoke.

I don't think any harm'll come to me... not for now.

Trust no one.

'You're welcome here, Maklan. You made it through the wood, no blood drawn. Eat, you get shelter for one night. In the morning... you go, no questions. Mess us around and you'll get a proper beating. Doesn't get any clearer.'

Something's wrong with this place... can feel it in my bones.

CHAPTER FIVE

SERRA OF THE RIVER TRIBE

It is so dark. It smells of animals and heat and stinking boys. When I get out of here there will be war against these people... these nasty children.

If you get out, Serra.

I will get out and they will pay for what they've done to me.

How will you get out of here? You can't even move, you can't stand up, you can't move your hands, you can't see or speak. They'll be back and they'll do it again... there's nothing you can do to stop it.

Move your legs.

They tied me up too well. The binding is cutting into my skin. My hands... what have they done to my hands? I can't feel them... numb, they're tied behind my back, strapped up so tight. I can't feel my legs, arms, feet, hands... the blood's stopped flowing.

Someone's coming. Outside. Boys talking to each other, laughing, play fighting. Please don't bring them in here... not again. Stay still. Don't move.

Where are you Lorkan? Where are you when I need you most, brother and father, my people? Where are you? You must know I'm here. Why haven't you come to get me? I could die here, in this stinking animal hut at the hands of these monsters. Please, please, please someone come.

Your tribe think you are hunting, Serra. It could be days before they send a search party.

The only way you're going to get out of here is if you do it yourself. Forget about your tribe, your family. You're on your own and you know it.

All I wanted was rabbit or otter. And this is what the gods give me. In this darkness. Waiting for them to come back again. I should never have gone out alone.

There were too many of them.

You did everything you could. You'll get out of here. Your luck will change. I can feel it.

Try to sleep. If I can't get out in body maybe the dream spirits will take me home. Back to my fire, to my mother's broth, father, brother, my bed.

The ground is so hard, I will never get any sleep on this ground. Breathe, breathe deep. Like the elder women showed you. Breathe into your belly... calm yourself. Close your eyes. Try and sleep.

So hungry, thirsty... tired.

Home. Remember home. That last night by the fire; father showing Lorkan how to restring his bow. Lorkan watching his every move like his life depended on it. Father's hands around the gut string, pulling it tight through the slit at the top, tying it fast. The fire lighting his work, glinting off the bowstring making it look like a thin streak of flame against the black sky.

Father had shown me how to string a bow and fire an arrow straight and true two summers before, round that same fire. Father never sees the difference between me and Lorkan. Only age separates us, which means I get to learn everything before my brother.

You are a good man, Farlan of the River Tribe, a good father. If you were here now you would teach these monsters a lesson they would never forget. You would carry me home in your arms and mother would feed me and bathe me and give me new clothes. Perhaps one day I would forget this ever happened to me.

No.

I will never forget this.

Here...

...sleep at last.

Sleep Serra.

Sleep.

Chapter Six

LOST BOYS

'You, rat boy. Come with us.'

'Where we going?' *Just go with them, Maklan.*

'You'll see.'

Food. Can smell it, meat... rabbit. They're cooking rabbit. Huts look new. Not solid like back home, these are made of willow, ash and reeds. Mud slapped on and dried hard to keep the wind out. Most of the doorways open to the weather. None made good. Just there to keep the rain and the wind off. Wind could just blow them over or fire sparks could burn them to ashes.

Can't see any women.

No mothers, wise women, no men older than twenty summers. They're all my age. All with worn out, dirty faces. But they look fit, mean, well-fed, strong. They get fed and I don't.

Here come two of them. Maybe they have some food? Don't see them carrying anything.

They're taking me to the edge of the village. Maybe they lied to me. Chucking me out without giving me any food.

Weird looking hut. Doorway all blocked up. Walls look like they are falling apart.

'You'll sleep there, with the dogs, they're all bitches. If you're feeling the need of a woman, sure one of them will help out.'

What's that sound in there, in the hut? Something else in there. An animal? Sounds like it's in pain. Something feels bad in there.

'There's food round the fire, come and eat.'

Something's wrong with this place. Apart from the lack of older men and women.

Leading me back to the fire. Food.

———

Leader has warriors either side, protecting him. Don't like the look of the skinny one, madness in his eyes, and that other one, big, solid, mean-looking. He's the shadow from the wood. No doubt.

Someone's bringing me food. At last.

'What is it?'

'Just eat.'

Looks alright.

What are they looking at? Never seen a man eat before? Leader looks like he's going to speak.

'Had another one like you from the north – two days ago. Came from the same tribe as you.'

Sanfar? 'He have a name?'

'Sin something. Sinfar.'

'Sanfar.' *He's been here.*

'That was it. Sanfar. Sent him to the Hill. Thought I'd put him through the same senseless game I went through. You know him, this Sanfar?'

'A little. Where is this hill?'

'The Hill's not a place, he's a man, old, more than a hundred summers some say. Plenty leave the village to seek him out, none've returned, except me.'

'Who is he?'

'Just a man. Lives in a wood two-days' walk from here with his wolfhound. People say he's wise. I say he's a fool. Walked for two days to find some wise words. He hardly spoke, just looked at me and asked one stupid question then went silent.'

'What was the question?'

'Asked me if I was ready.'

'Ready for what?' *Give them your bowl; maybe they'll fill it up.*

'Just if I was ready, not what for. Left his hut cursing the fool's waste of my time and headed back. I have no questions need answering. All I need I have here.'

'Where are the women... the elders?'

'No need for them. If we want a woman we go to the next valley and take one, burn a few huts to warm us up and bring her back for as long as we need.'

'You take women from other tribes?'

There's that sound again. Coming from my hut. 'Why are you here with only young men and boys for a tribe?'

'Here. Drink. It's good.'

Mead. This is the stuff that turns father into a monster. Never drunk it before. Never been this thirsty before. 'Why are you here?'

'Same reason as you.'

'I haven't told you why I'm here.'

'You told my chief warrior that you have no tribe. We are alike in that. None of us have tribes. We've left our villages. Sworn never to return.'

'Why?'

'Because none of us have fathers. They're either dead from battle, moved to other tribes without word, or they beat us when the drink is in their skin. Came here because we can't trust the men who are supposed to protect us and teach us. So we protect ourselves, teach ourselves, feed ourselves and entertain ourselves.'

Mead feels good. Warming me up. 'What you do… that's the job of the elders. Everyone knows that.'

'There are not men enough to hold us. When they come maybe we will follow them. Maybe not. Maybe we'll just fight.'

There's a deadness in his eyes. Fire isn't warming me any more. Neither is the mead. Maybe if I have some more. No. That's why Sanfar drinks… the fear.

This place is dangerous… I must leave…

… at daybreak.

Chapter Seven

LIGHT BREAKING

Wake up, Serra. Wake up. Someone is in here with me. I can hear him breathing. He's asleep, he's not coming for me, just sleeping.

I didn't hear him come in. I slept right through. How long have I been asleep? I still can't feel my legs or arms. I must move. Light is breaking through the hut walls, the roof, the doorway. It must be sunny outside. Warm. Sunshine outside, freedom... and all this darkness and coldness in here.

Wiggle your fingers, Serra, your toes, nose.

Nothing.

If I lie here much longer I'm going to die.

I must move.

I'm not going to die here and I'm not going let any of them come near me again.

How are you going stop them?

Why won't someone come and get me?!

CHAPTER EIGHT

SHAPE SHIFTER

The black shape moves through the mist toward Maklan, the milky white blanket wiping out everything beyond the gnarled hawthorn in front of him. The silhouetted shape begins to take form. A black outline, an outline Maklan recognises. He knows every line and contour of it, a walk he has seen many times before...

The figure continues to walk toward him. He knows who this human is.

'SANFAR!!' He calls out. 'Found you!!'

Sanfar walks out of the mist-covered moor, spear in hand, a look of blackness and anger on his face. Maklan knows something is wrong. Something has changed. Sanfar is coming straight for him. He is dirty, bloodied from some kind of battle, a deep cut on his cheek, a horrible limp. His left arm looks wrecked, maybe broken, twisted at a sickening right angle, a small round of white bone sticking out of the scabbed flesh and muscle of his forearm. He stumbles toward Maklan, eyes wild with madness inside, but he doesn't see him, he looks straight through him, beyond him, into a place beyond this world.

'Brother!' The half-muted, shocked words fall from Maklan's mouth in a frightened whisper.

There is death and coldness in Sanfar's eyes. Maklan wants to run to his tribe-brother, greet him, hug him and speak to him, but his feet are rooted to the marshy ground.

Rain falls steadily through the whited-out, silent landscape, a thin, non-stop drizzle saturating Maklan's clothes, hair and face. He is cold.

Sanfar keeps walking, stumbling, hobbling toward him slamming his bare feet down into the uneven ground to stop himself from falling. He gets closer, his footfall heavier, he begins to slow down. The mist and fog swirl around him, hiding and revealing his body like the soft blurring hand of a giant dark magician. His legs and arms and face become darker. Maklan wants to shout out to him, a warning. But no sound comes from his mouth.

Hair begins to sprout through Sanfar's muddied, bloodied skin, animal hair, long, coarse, reddish brown. Hands and feet begin to transform, mutate into something beyond human... black, thick, the hooves of a beast. Maklan tries to take a step back but he cannot move his feet. Sanfar gets closer by the second. Maklan feels horror rise in him as he watches his tribe-brother shapeshift from human into some kind of twisted, broken animal.

Sanfar's skull begins to tremble and shimmer like rising heat vapour off sun-burnt rock.

'Sanfar!'

Thick, dark blood trickles down Sanfar's face creating a glistening crimson death mask. His eyes sink back into his skull and are slowly replaced by deep black orbs.

Maklan throws up on his feet with fear. He wipes his mouth and looks up and sees the rising bone of antler push up through his tribe-brother's scalp. The thin skull skin rips and tears. He continues to stumble toward Maklan. As he gets closer the antlers grow, like the fingering branches of a leafless tree. Sanfar falls forward onto all fours, completing the transformation from human to animal. Maklan now knows this animal, the sacred animal of forest and moor... the wild stag.

The huge animal begins to canter toward a now paralysed, petrified Maklan.

Stag-human at full charge, Maklan shuts his eyes... and prepares for impact.

Nothing.

Only silence.

No fear.

Silence.

CHAPTER NINE

ESCAPE

Wake up Maklan. Mouth dry, rank. What is that taste?

Where am I? Can't see a thing.

Place stinks. The hut. I'm in the dogs' hut. How in Thunor's name did I get here?

Mead. You drank a lot of mead last night. My head... banging like a hammer. That smell, think I'm going to throw up. Shouldn't be here. Mouth feels like dung. Must get water. Need to get back to the woods, the river, keep moving. Find Sanfar. Bring him back.

What was that dream? Sanfar changing into some kind of stag?

Stupid nightmare. Nothing to be scared of.

Thought it was real.

How much did I drink?

Lost count at ten.

Back, neck killing me, can't move it properly.

Remember getting up, lost the use of me legs... think I passed out before I hit the ground.

They must have carried me here.

Wish I'd slept outside... under the stars.

Dogs keeping their distance, staying out of sight in the corner shadows.

Wait.

There's something else in here... in the shadows, over in the far corner.

There it is again... that sound from last night.

I knew something was wrong.

Oh Thunor. No.

I know what it is... the sound missing... from the camp. That's what's in the corner...

... a woman.

Sounds like she's in pain... scared, broken, beaten. 'Who's over there? Say something. I'm not going to hurt you. Say something... please...'

'That's what you all say.'

'What? What do they all say? Who?

'You say you're not going to hurt me... but you do... every time.'

'I'm not from this village. I came here last night. Who hurts you?'

'If you're not from here then get me out... take me back to my tribe. Get me away from this these animals pretending to be men.'

I know why she's here... in the corner. They were talking about it round the fire last night. They laughed about it. All I did was get drunk and pass out. I know why she's cowering in the corner. Get out... now, Maklan. Get out.

Take her with you.

Too dangerous. She'll slow me down. Not my responsibility.

You can't leave her here. It is your responsibility and you know it.

They'll come after me. If I go alone they'll leave me alone.

She's moving. Coming into the light. Crawling.

Her face... bruised, lip... torn, scabbed. Hair matted with mud and twigs and... blood. Hands and feet tied. Nothing covering her body. What have they done to her?

Give her your deerskin.

'Thank you.'

'Can you run?'

'I don't know. Untie me.'

Blade. Cut her ropes and get out of here. 'You need to rub your legs, get the flow of blood back.'

'I can't move my hands properly...numb.'

'Come into the light. I'll rub your legs, you get your arms. We have to get out of here. The village is waking up.'

Be gentle with her.

'Can you stand?'

'I'll soon find out.'

'Give me your hand. Hold on. Don't let go.'

Thunor, the light is bright out here. Head still screaming. 'Keep low. Are your legs good enough to run?'

'No, not really. I could crawl.'

'Can you get on my back?'

'I think so.'

She's lighter than I thought. Good. I've strength enough. Now Maklan... RUN!

CHAPTER TEN

THE RIVER

Maklan moves round the huts as silent as the earth with Serra on his back. The village is asleep. They make it to the boundary. He stops for breath.

He runs again, Serra holding him tight, praying for freedom.

The sound of the river quickly reaches them and they head for it.

When they get to its banks they drink. Maklan washes his face. Serra takes off his deerskin and walks, slow, unsteady, naked, silent, into the water up to her waist and begins to wash herself. Slowly at first, as in a ritual. She begins to rock back and forth. A low moan builds in her throat as she scrubs her body clean of dirt and blood with her bare hands. A low cry of pain and anguish begins to rise from her. She scrubs harder, now trying to remove unseen dirt. Her hands dip beneath the water to wash the place of violation. She begins to cry. A wail of utter anguish and sorrow that Maklan has never heard the like of. A sound that will scar his memory forever.

'You must keep quiet.' He pleads. 'If they hear us they will come and they will do worse to us.'

Serra shoots him a look of rage. 'Nothing is worse than what they've done to me. You will never know it. They stole something very precious from me.' She ducks her head under the water and disappears. Maklan can just hear the muffled, liquid scream come from under the surface of the fast-moving river. It's carried by the rush and rumble of water on rock, downstream. He is sickened by the raw, primeval sound. He knows she must do this and knows she can't be heard beyond the banks of the river. She has to cleanse herself but he wishes it would stop.

After a full two minutes Serra rises up out of the water. Her face and hair clear of mud and dirt. Maklan turns his head away from her naked body. She wades to the bank and puts his deerskin back on. She looks at him, anger and pain still in her eyes. She sits and wraps her arms round herself, shivering. She looks over to him. Maklan thinks he can see the rise of a half smile on her face. A smile of thanks. He can see her beauty now. The beauty that drew the boy tribe to take her. The beauty few could resist.

But he will.

CHAPTER ELEVEN

STORM CATCHER

Maklan wonders how long they will sit there in silence. He wishes she would say something. 'How are your legs?'

'Good; better, thank you.'

'Do you know where the Hill is?'

'What hill?' She breaks off a small piece of ivy vine and ties her hair back with it.

'Not what, who. He's an old man. I'm looking for my tribe-brother, Sanfar, they said he went to him and I need to find him.'

'Jacob Hill you mean. My father knows him. I'll show you how to get there you if you promise to protect me.'

'I'm not about to stop now.'

'I live half a days walk from him. We'll part before we get to his hut Hill. I'll show you how to get there. I will draw you a map in the earth.'

'Thank you. What's your name?'

'Why?'

'Just thought it would be good to know; in case we get into trouble and I need to get your attention.'

'You have my attention – I know what you're going to do before you do.'

'Just trying to be friendly.'

'Sorry. My name is Serra. You?'

'Maklan. Storm Catcher.'

Serra chuckles to herself.

'What's funny?'

'What kind of a name is Storm Catcher?'

Maklan is embarrassed and irritated at the same time. 'Sanfar gave it to me. It's my elemental name. We gave each other names when we were hunting three seasons ago. There was a hurricane, biggest I'd seen and I...

'Let me guess. You caught it... and stuck it in your pocket? Not the brightest thing to do, chasing a hurricane. That kind of thing can get you killed.'

'Well I'm alive.' He tries not to stare at her. 'What's your tribe name?'

'Sun Catcher, River Tribe.'

'You chase the sun then do you?' Maklan smiles at her smugly.

'Don't be stupid.'

'Storm Catcher and Sun Catcher, must be a sign.'

'Maklan, I need to be clear with you. You and your blade are protecting me till I get you to the Hill. I'm thankful for that, truly I am. But there are no signs, just a chance meeting, nothing more.' Serra smells the air and looks behind her. 'We must go. They're coming. I can smell that boy stink ten leagues away. Those dogs in that hut will know my scent by heart. We need to cross the river... the water will cover our tracks and scent. That is where we will lose them.'

'You lead the way. I'll keep a look out behind.' Maklan stands up and looks around.

Serra picks up a thick stick and pulls off the smaller branches. 'Give me your blade.'

Maklan hands it to her. She quickly sharpens the stick and hands the blade back. 'Keep your blade out. They're sneaky and fast. They surrounded me before I even knew they were there. We must move fast, keep low and don't stop running till I do.'

'You lead the way.'

CHAPTER TWELVE

HUNTED

Maklan and Serra run nonstop through the rough terrain. Sweat drips from their brows and down their backs. They stop briefly here and there to eat berries, sorrel, pignuts, moorland herbs, any fruit they can find on tree or bush. It isn't enough but it keeps them going. Maklan feels the constant threat of being hunted down by the boy tribe. He looks back over his shoulder so often his neck begins to hurt. He uses his knowledge of birdcalls to warn him of any danger from behind. The birds alarm call to one another ahead of Maklan and Serra as they run. If birdcalls come from behind they will have to hide. It is the only warning they have.

No such warnings come.

Comfortable with the distance they have covered between this point and the boys' village, Maklan watches Serra as she scans the ground and the tree line ahead.

'What you looking for?'

'Food. More than berries. Meat.'

'There's nothing to hunt round here.'

'Give me your knife.'

Maklan takes out his blade without question and hands it to her.

Serra slows her pace, stops and crouches down. She gestures back to Maklan to do the same. He follows.

Ahead is a cluster of beech trees rising into the sky. Bright green spring leaves move like a million fat little fingers in the wind. At the base of the trees a series of small black rabbit holes. Serra gets lower, almost to a crawl. Maklan stops, waits and watches. She pushes her belly to the ground and crawls as close as she can, then stops.

She waits.

The wind blows cool into Maklan's face. He can see she is a natural-born hunter, easy with the landscape.

Then she does something he hasn't seen before. She gently sinks his blade into the ground so as not to disturb anything, takes off the ivy holding her hair up and ties it around the handle. Her hair falls about her shoulders. She brings her hand to her heart; her lips begin to move as she says a silent prayer to herself, the land and the spirits.

She continues to pray for some time. Maklan becomes bored. He lies on the hard ground, closes his eyes and drifts into a broken sleep.

———

The spattering of warm liquid on Maklan's face wakes him up. He snaps open his eyes and sees the dead rabbit, blood dripping from its nose, hanging above him, back legs held tight in Serra's hand. He moves quickly out of the way and wipes his face.

'What are you doing?!'

Serra grins down at Maklan. 'Now we can eat some proper food.'

They build a fire with bone-dry thistle, bracken and standing dead wood.

Maklan takes out his fire-making kit and prepares a fire.
Serra guts the rabbit.

They cook over a low flame in silence. Knowing the risk they take in fire smoke being seen by those who hunt them. Their hunger makes it a risk worth taking.

It is the best food Maklan has eaten in days.

'What were you doing earlier?' he asks, licking his fingers.

'When?'

'When you were on the ground... waiting for the rabbit.'

'Praying. Do you not do that, when you're hunting?'

Maklan shrugs his shoulders. 'We do a ceremony before we go out but not when we're on the hunt. Never time for that.'

'It's no good just doing a ceremony in your village. You need to do it on the land you're hunting on.'

'What if your prey comes in the middle of a prayer?'

'They don't.' Serra scans Maklan, looking for something. He shifts uncomfortably. 'Why did you leave your village?'

'Told you. Looking for my tribe-brother, Sanfar.'

'You really think I'm that stupid?'

'No.'

'You're out here for more than that. I can see it on you, it's all over you, it's in your eyes. You have that hunted look. I would know it anywhere. Looks like you need some prayers yourself.'

Maklan looks down at the ground. 'I'm tired. Need to sleep.'

Serra spreads the embers of the fire. All smoke now gone.

They prepare their beds under an overhanging rock. They put down dry moss and cover themselves with fresh-cut bracken. The embers keep the front of their bodies warm. Their backs remain chilled. They lie close enough to keep the rest of their bodies warm, but far enough apart for Serra not to feel threatened.

Maklan constantly shifts his position to stop his back from hurting or the tips of deeply buried rocks poking and jabbing into his skin. He drifts into sleep with painful, sharp memories of the last night in his village.

Chapter Thirteen

WOLF AT THE DOOR

A quarter moon before

This roof needs fixing, moonlight coming in, keeping me awake.

> It isn't the moon keeping you awake, Maklan.

Never sleep good when the moon's full.

> It isn't the moon.

Mother always said, 'If the moon can move the tides in the ocean, it can move the blood in our bodies. No wonder it turns people into lunatics.'

> There's one lunatic be back soon enough.

It was good tonight, with Tenmar and Farrar, the best brother and sister I could wish for. And mother. Good eating, talking, sitting by the fire. There was some peace here, with him out there.

> That will soon be broken.

There it is. Wolf on the moor. Calling to its brothers, maybe its mate. I'd be out there with them, if I could. Live with the wolves, if they'd take me. Better than this. This isn't a home. Besides, they would probably eat me soon as look at me.

He's later than usual.

He'll be back soon enough and he'll be full of wine and anger. Same old story. Always this way. Ribs only just recovering from the last beating.

Don't give him any more lip. Don't fight back this time.

Please let him be too drunk to fight or strike, too drunk to do anything except sleep. Keep him away from mother... from all of us. Thunor, keep him away.

Your prayers are useless, you know that.

Footsteps. He's coming. Staggering. Not crashing into anything. Not drunk enough.

He's in. Trying to be quiet. Everyone will be awake now.

Get up. Head him off. Maybe he's drunk enough to push him over then you can put him to sleep with your stick.

Then what? What will you do after that... in the morning when he wakes? He'll break every bone in your body.

Listen. He's heading to Farrar's sleeping place. Wait. He's stopped by mother's place. He's trying to make his mind up which one to go to.

I must do something. 'Tenmar! Wake up. He's back and he's gone to Farra!'

'I'm awake, brother. What do you want me to do?'

'Come with me. We can stop him together.'

'And deal with his punishment for the next two moons? Forget it.'

'So we just leave her? We can't leave her... we have to help her!!'

Tenmar sits up in bed. 'We been here too many times, brother. I have no more ideas. Maybe he'll fall asleep before it starts. '

'Come with me.'

'No.'

'Not going to let him do it again. I'll go alone. He can kick the life out of me if he likes. Not letting him do that to her again. You'll regret it more if you do nothing.'

'Wait. I'm coming. We're going to regret this.'

'No we won't.' *Slow, foot down gentle on the ground. You know how to get through this hut without being heard, Maklan. Get to him before he gets to her. Before he does any more damage.*

Chapter Fourteen

THIEF

How long is this boy going to sleep? He keeps me awake half the night snoring and now he's just lying there on his back with a grin on his face like a puppy dog. I gathered the wood, lit the fire, cooked the rest of the rabbit. Men!

The puppy is stirring, Serra. 'You're awake then. I thought you might be dead for a minute.'

'Enough of that for me?'

'We will both get an even share.'

'I feel like death. Slept badly. This ground is too hard, too dry.'

'You could have fooled me. You snored all night.'

'I don't snore. I had nightmares.'

'You were talking in your sleep.'

'What did I say?'

'Mumbling most of the time. You kept saying his name over and over.'

'Whose name?'

'Sanfar.' *Ask him, Serra.*

It's none of my business.

It's why he's here. Why he's come all this way Ask him. 'What happened?'

'With what?'

'Sanfar. Apart from running around chasing storms and girls.'

'Sanfar stole from our village winter stores.'

'What did he steal?'

'Wine.'

'He drinks for a reason.'

'There's always a reason... getting drunk is pretty high on the list.'

He's stopped speaking. He's looking at the ground. I think I upset him.

Apologise.

Don't put him in the same hole as all the others. He is trying to help. Maklan is different, you can see that.

'I'm sorry. That was wrong of me.'

'It's alright.'

'Have you ever stolen?'

'I stole honey once... from the hives at the end of the village. When I was five summers old. Father beat me so hard I couldn't sit down for a week. Haven't stolen since.'

'Why did you do it?'

'I like honey.'

'Maybe that's why Sanfar stole... because it's nice, because he liked it.'

'Sanfar didn't just like it... he drank it all the time... he needed it. I never tried it till the other night. That was mead. Honey. Tasted good. Sanfar was always trying to get me to drink it, but I saw what it did to him... and my father. Turned them both into dangerous idiots.'

I feel safe around you, Maklan of the Deer Tribe. You seem strong. A handsome man. Good cheekbones. Strong shoulders. 'He must be special to you, Sanfar... to come all the way out here.'

'I'd die for him. He's saved my life twice and I'd do anything to return that. He needs to come back to the village. He needs to be forgiven. He did what he did for a reason. He's a good brother, a good warrior and a good hunter.'

'They say it takes one to know one.'

'Who says?'

'The elders.' *Be kind to him, Serra.*

He'll make a good husband to someone one day, a good father, maybe even a good hunter. He has the mark of a leader about him.

'We need to get moving. The rain is coming.'

Chapter Fifteen

THE HILL

Maklan and Serra emerge into open moorland. Serra points down to the mass of trees stretching out for leagues in every direction.

'Jacob Hill lives in there. You'll find him easily; follow the smell of wood-smoke. He always has a fire going.' She takes off the deerskin and hands it back to Maklan. 'I've changed my mind. I'll head back alone... I can make it on my own. They won't come this far. Thank you for everything.'

'You can't go back on your own and you can't go back like that.'

She smiles back at him. 'I'm warm enough from walking and the sun is still high. I want to go back to my village like this, so my tribe will know what those children did to me. Then there will be many fires in the boy tribe village.'

Maklan doesn't respond. He takes his deerskin from her and puts it back on. He reaches out his hand to take hers. She refuses it, instead walking up to him and hugging him.

'Thank you for protecting me, Maklan. You are a good man. I'll make sure you're not hurt.' Serra turns and walks down the valley. Maklan watches her leave and immediately wishes she was still with him.

'Wait!' He runs up to her. 'I'm coming with you. Not letting you walk back like that. I promised to protect you and we agreed I'd walk you back to your village.'

Serra smiles at him without replying and nods.

They continue walking together in silence.

———

They come to the crest of the hill leading down to Serra's village. They look down in silence. She takes hold of his hand and squeezes it.

'I don't want you to come down with me. I want to walk the last stretch home alone.'

'Then I'll stay here and wait till you're through the gate.'

'That's up to you.' She lets go of his hand. 'We'll see each other again, I know that.' She embraces him and kisses him on the cheek. She turns and heads down the hill.

Maklan watches her every step. Her bruised, naked back getting more and more distant as she moves closer to home. A small black dog comes out of the village gate first and runs up to her. She bends down and strokes it.

One by one, villagers come out to greet her. An older woman walks up to her and puts her arms round her. In a short time Serra is surrounded, protected by a large gathering of villagers who lead her back home, to safety. When the last of the villagers is back within the high stone and wood walls, Maklan breathes out a long sigh, turns and heads back for Jacob Hill's land.

———

It takes Maklan the best part of two hours to work his way through the scrub and boulders and marshland and thickset trees.

In places his legs sink hip-deep into the boggy, sodden ground. Midges, flies and mosquitoes gnaw into him leaving irritating bites. He scratches them till they bleed. The edges of the wood are thick with a mass of thin, spindly trees and dense, thorn-spiked bushes. He cuts his arms and legs in a dozen places as he makes his way slowly through. All the time following the direction of the faint smell of wood-smoke.

———

It's late afternoon when he finally comes to the clearing. At the edge of it is a small hut with a thin wisp of grey smoke creeping into a white sky. He walks toward it, starving and tired. Before he gets halfway across the open space the door of the hut opens and a large wolfhound trots silently out and heads straight for him. He steps back, afraid he'll be bitten, but the dog just sniffs at him.

A figure appears at the door and watches them. The dog turns and heads back to the entrance of the hut. The man leans down as if speaking to the animal then looks back up at Maklan. He beckons him forward. Maklan obeys.

As he reaches the hut he slows down, cautious. 'Are you... are you Jacob Hill?'

'I am. And you are?' The man's voice is old, but strong with humour.

'Maklan, Storm Chaser of the Deer Tribe. I come from the north. I'm looking for my tribe-brother, Sanfar.'

'That's quite a name. Come... come inside.' Jacob smiles at him. 'Looks like you lost the war with my marsh bugs. You need medicine for those bites, they're small but they're poisonous and they scar if you scratch them.'

Maklan looks at him alarmed, stops scratching his arms, rubs his face and walks past the dog, into the warmth and heat of the hut. He smells soup cooking and his stomach instantly rumbles.

'I've soup and bread if you're hungry?' Maklan nods. 'Sit.' The old man prepares the food and brings it over. The wolfhound finds himself a place by the fire, turns a few times and lies down. The old man sits down opposite Maklan and smiles warmly. He leans over to a wooden box and takes out a leather pouch. Maklan watches him, eating quickly, letting the food warm him. The insect bites begin to sting again. Jacob unrolls the pouch laying out a cluster of small clay bottles. He takes two out, reaches for a pestle and mortar and pours half of each bottle into the pestle. He begins to grind the herbs down, adding spit as he goes.

'Have you seen my tribe-brother... Sanfar?'

'Why have you come here?'

Maklan is surprised by the question. 'I'm looking for my warrior brother, my tribe-brother... Sanfar.'

'But why have *you* come here, to me? Looks like you've travelled a long way.'

'I'm looking...' Maklan's reply trails off and he goes silent. Jacob Hill looks at him long and hard.

'You're not just looking for your brother. There's something more pushing you.'

'I'm sorry... I don't understand...'

Jacob looks at him without expression. 'Your heart's closed, boy, that's clear enough.' It's not a question. It's a statement. Maklan becomes agitated. He wants to leave but his belly isn't full.

'Your heart's closed and you're blind. Someone has stolen your fire, Maklan of the Deer Tribe.' Jacob smiles. He finishes the herb grinding and hands the bowl to Maklan. 'Put this on your bites. It will stop the itching, stop any poison getting into your blood and help with the scarring.'

'I'm not putting that on my face. You just spat into it!'

'Suit yourself.'

Maklan takes the herbs and looks suspiciously at the ointment. 'What do you mean my heart is closed?'

'You know well enough.' Jacob sits back in his chair.

'Don't know what you're talking about. I'm looking for my tribe-brother and I was told he came here. If you won't answer my question... I'll go.'

'No need to sulk, boy. You're not here simply for your tribe-brother. We both know that.'

Maklan puts the herbs down and stands. 'Thank you for the soup and the fire. I need to make shelter before nightfall.' He heads for the door, the dog remains asleep. As he reaches the threshold Jacob speaks. 'If the young aren't initiated into the tribe, they will burn down the village just to feel its warmth.' He looks at Maklan for a long moment. 'You'll know the true meaning of blindness before the night is out.'

Without saying another word, Maklan walks out of the hut filled with anger and disappointment.

He walks back into the forest, stomping ahead, raging at having come so far just to be asked stupid questions.

He scratches his itching, burning skin but it makes no difference. *Let them scar. See if I care.*

The hunger in his belly rises again and he quickly begins to wish he'd stayed longer, asked for another bowl of soup and taken the medicine. He hungers for meat. The rabbit Serra caught was good but not enough. He needs red meat to sustain him, the meat of his tribe, the meat of deer.

He moves into the forest and begins to look for signs of deer tracks. His hunting skills are good despite what his father says, maybe good enough to kill his first deer, maybe a small one. If he's lucky he may find one before nightfall – if not he will look for signs of where they sleep and try and take one before it wakes.

———

Maklan walks deep into the moor, further and further away from Jacob, the wolfhound, Serra, the Lost Boy Tribe, his village and warm food. He hopes and prays he is getting closer to Sanfar.
He searches the ground for deer tracks.

Days now separate him from the place he was born and grew up. He has travelled further now than he ever had with Sanfar on their hunting trips. His isolation and loneliness grow. He sees fewer and fewer animals. He looks for the tracks of deer and finds none. The light has almost gone and the fear in him grows as the darkness approaches.

'Why are you here?' Jacob's question repeats over and over, eating into his mind.

'Your heart is closed and you are blind.'

What in Thunor's name did he mean by that? Old fool. Knows nothing about me and thinks he can just tell me what he likes? The leader was right, he is a fool. Wasted my time. Even his broth was tasteless.

Maklan knows why he left his village. He is driven forward by his past with no clear picture of where he is headed. He knows for sure he is utterly lost.

Chapter Sixteen

DON'T LOOK BACK

Don't look back, Serra.

This walk... to the village, so familiar... the ground, the way it dips and lifts. I know every bit of it. I could walk through this blindfold and not trip once. But something has changed. It doesn't feel the same. Everything has changed.

Keep walking, Serra.

Don't look back.

I can smell the fire, cooking. Laughing. Screaming. Fun. That will be the children playing by the chief's hut. He hates that.

Cold. The wind is cold on my skin.

Keep walking.

I should've taken his deerskin.

Then he would've been cold. He has a far longer way to go. You've only a few more yards.

I think I'm going to miss him.

Keep walking.

Something's coming to the gate. A small black dog. Is it? Yes ... !!

'Kera? Kera! Come here girl. Come here. Thunor, it's good to see you! You're skinny, you need feeding.'

People coming. Why are they walking so slowly? Why aren't they running?

You're half naked, your wounds can be seen. They're afraid.

As you would be.

Mother is there... at the back, and father, coming for me. Lorkan? Where's Lorkan?

So many of them, it seems like all of them, everyone. Everyone in the village is coming to greet me.

My legs... so weak. What is happening to my legs? It feels like they are giving way.

Let go, Serra. You're home. You can let go now. You're safe. You're home.

———

'Bring her in. Carry her. Don't crowd her. Give her some room, let her breathe, give her some room to breathe.'

'I don't need carrying.'

'What's happened to her!?'

So many voices, I know them, my tribe. Everyone is here. My family, my village. Everyone...mother, her hands... on mine. Father's... round my shoulders, strong, warm, safe.

'Why is she naked,?'

Child's voice. Marlan's child.

'Someone give her a skin to cover her.'

'How did you get those marks, Serra?'

The village elder... Nasa. She's here, even she has come to greet me. My knees... so weak.

'Serra, you are in so much trouble, woman!! Where have you been?!'

'Rasra! Thunor, your voice is music to my ears. I knew you would be here.'

'Where have you been, Serra? You've been gone for days! Everyone has been looking for you. Out of the way. Make way, let her come through, she's not a ghost! Stop staring! She needs rest and healing. What happened, Serra? How did you get all those marks on your body?'

Arms round me. Holding me. I have missed this so much. Don't let her go. Don't ever let her go. My legs... giving way, can't stand any more. So tired.

'Someone come and help me carry her in.'

'I walked back. I can walk back through my village gates.'

'Give her something to cover her!'

Legs giving way.

'What happened to her, father? Why does she look so sad?'

'I don't know, child.'

So many people. Time to rest, Serra. Time to rest.

'Get her into the village. She needs medicine and rest. Then we find out who did this.'

'It's alright, Serra. I'll take care of you.'

'Thank you, Rasra.'

CHAPTER SEVENTEEN

SILVERINE

The skinny, disheveled young man stands in front of the open stall staring down at the cakes, biscuits and pies. His stomach grumbles in protest, pushing him, nagging, hassling. Only water's passed his dry shriveled lips in the last three days, and dirty water at that. Water from dark river pools and puddles, rain-filled, insect-riddled barrels with rotting wood floating on their murky surfaces. He ate some of the insects last night. The worms made him want to throw up before they even passed his lips. The smell of deep, black earth on their writhing, glistening bodies made him want to vomit with regret, and anger, burning, endless anger, and bitterness. He tried to catch bigger animals but his once sharp hunting skills have gone. His razor sense of the wild vanished, replaced and matched by the empty, soullessness of this dark, sprawling, settlement of huts and shacks and dirty mud-filled streets; its wooden ramshackle outhouses, bridges, narrow dirt paths, half-lit lanes reeking of danger, double-dealing and fear. The fear and madness forcing brother to fight brother in every shit-stinking corner of the place they call Heartfall. This once proud dwelling place; gateway to the western lands, this place of rich trade, place of welcome to all nations, religions, creeds, colours and size of pocket is eating itself with madness and terror and greed. Its wooden carts and wagons and caravans roll in and out of the crumbling high wooden walls, day and night, nonstop, looking for business, loaded with half-rotting food and powerful, cheap, mind-numbing drink, expensive spices and moth-eaten cloth. These same rattling wooden vehicles leave by cover of night piled high with bodies for the marshlands. The bodies of children and men and women fallen prey to Heartfall's vices, death and disease.

The young man looks up, refocusing on his blurred reflection in the dull battered bronze tray half-full of pies: patchy, stubbly, goaty beard, not the hair of a man but a boy. Face streaked with so much dirt his eyes are the only part of his metal reflection he can clearly see. Dead eyes. Life beaten out of them. He clenches his long, blackened nails, digging them deep into the palms of his hands, using anger and bitterness to force him into doing something. Fingernails sink into the skin of his palm. The skin tightens and begins to split, rip, tear. Warm blood seeps slowly into his clenched fists. The warmth reassures him. The pain that follows, the pain he knew would come, is the pain he needs to wake him up from his hunger-induced stupor, to get him moving. He blinks, breathes in sharply through his nose and looks up at the stallholder.

The old woman gives him a half smile, empty of meaning. 'Morning dear. What can I get for you?'

He doesn't answer. He just looks at the food, dazed and confused. Thick drops of blood fall slowly from his fists onto a pie. Deep crimson on the pastry of the cooked wheat 'You're bleeding. You alright, dear? What you done to your hands?'

He reaches for the biggest pie. Three more dark globules of blood fall onto a pile of freshly baked pies. He is momentarily transfixed, watching the liquid from his pain-wracked body fall in slow motion, splashing, one, two, three onto the food. He reaches down, fingers encircling a bloodied pie.

'Now look what you've done! No chance of selling these now is there?!' Her voice has shifted from soft concern to rising anger.

'Torfar... come out here, luv. We've another one.'

The young man hears the shift in her voice and knows what will follow will not be good. But he ignores it. Taking the big pie, he turns and begins to walk away. He hears the thudding boot step of someone big and purposeful coming up behind him. As he strides away from the stall he raises the blood-soaked pie to his cracked lips and takes a massive bite. His face aches with the stretch of it. Sunshine beats down and warms his face. His body responds rapidly to the food. In the fleeting moment it takes for him to cross the muddied lane, for the first time in weeks, a smile begins to break across his blackened face. He looks left and right for carts and walks into the hustle and bustle of horses and people. He is two steps from the opening to a darkened lane when he feels a mighty crack on the back of his head. His vision flicks to black. The pie falls from his hand. He is unconscious before his body hits the ground.

———

He opens his eyes; smells the air. He is lying on his back looking up at the thin bundle of reed and willow making up the roof of the small hut. The sound of the carts and horses from outside rattles through him. Someone is shouting at someone or something. Maybe a stubborn animal not moving. The hunger hits him again. His mouth is dry and rank and foul tasting. His head thumps. He hears someone come into the space. He sits up, stiffly.

The dark-skinned youth comes into view, grinning with malice. He holds out a half-eaten pie, dark, dried blood smeared across its surface.

'You owe us.' The dark youth sits down. 'You are lucky, brother.' He talks fast and frenetically. 'I was there. Saw it. Saw everything. Saw you take a bite out of this.' He looks at the pie as if it were amusing evidence. 'Then this big man comes with a big stick! Like he had a tree in his hand... gets it above his head and takes a swing and cracks you over the skull.' He gets up and starts pacing around the room getting more and more excited as the memory of the story unfolds. 'Clean shot. He must have been good at the game when he wasn't so fat - and ugly! You must have a thick skull. I thought your brains were going to come out your ears! You should have seen your face before you hit the mud!' He slaps his thigh, laughing at the memory. 'Pie in your hand, eyes big as plates like someone just told you they took your woman. Couldn't stop me laughing.' He continues to pace the room, waving his arms in the air. 'Then he stands over you raving about all the other ones like us who stole from him, then he looks up at me and shouts, "Let this be a lesson to any thief thinks he can steal MY pies!" And he starts waving that stick in the air and looks down at you like he's going to give you another crack. That's when I stepped in and told him everything was in order. I take out a bag of coin, ask him how much he wants for the pie and he looks at me, mouth hanging open, all sweaty, red in the face and looks down at you and starts scratching his chin. So I give him some coin, put the pie in my pocket and drag you up the street. You're heavy for a skinny one. Lucky I got muscle on me.' He finally sits down and looks at the young man and leans back against the wall. 'So... like I said, you owe us.'

The young man stands up. 'Thank you. Anything to drink?'

'Twice.'

'What do you mean, twice?'

'You owe us... twice, I saved your life twice, brother.'

'I don't get it.' He feels round the back of his head. The bloodied scab from the pieman's attack is thick, soft and moist. It stings.

He knows if he pushes it any harder, it will start bleeding. He wants to, but resists.

'Saved your life once from the pie man and once again from the noose... for thieving. That's the punishment for thieving in Heartfall. So that's twice. I saved your life twice. You owe us plenty.' The boy hands him the rest of the half-eaten pie.

The young thief knows what this means and his heart sinks. He wishes he were dead. He knows silverine will take this feeling away better than wine.

'You got some silverine, brother? I hear its good in Heartfall. Get me on my feet then I can thieve the coin I owe you.'

The boy looks at him, grinning. 'But you aren't such a good thief though, are you? Look at you. You don't want much, do you? I save you from a second beating, get your pie back for you and save you from the noose and now you want silverine! You've courage, give you that. Let's see what Zed has to say about it.' He stands up and heads out. He stops on the threshold and turns to look back. 'You know if Zed gets involved it'll cost you more... much more. What's your name?'

'Sanfar.'

'I'm Bones. Be captain Bones soon. Zed's right-hand man. Remember it.' Bones heads out of the room.

Sanfar takes a bite out of the hardening pie and slumps back on the bed. The wound stings and aches with the pressure of it. He looks up at the dim light coming through the gaps. Rain begins to fall hard and quickly drips onto him. He continues to chew on the pie, enjoying the taste of it as it slips in painful chunks down his throat.

The nagging hunger is quiet now. But there is a deep ache in his legs and arms, a throbbing in his head and a deep cold in his bones. The silverine sickness has taken over and is demanding to be fed.

Chapter Eighteen

TRUE BLINDNESS

Maklan's footfall is unsteady on the ground, feet constantly catching and clipping rocks and roots. He is so exhausted he's forgotten how hungry he is. The only signs of it now are his legs, weak and wobbly. He walks on, unclear which is the best direction, half his attention on deer tracking, the other half on his father, and his anger. If he were home now he'd burn the family hut to the ground – with his father in it. And the rest of village, for not protecting him from his father's drunken violence, he would burn their huts to the ground too. He'd stand on the edge of the village and watch it be eaten by flames... just so he could feel its warmth.

He walks into the last light of the day, to the highest part of the moor.

He misses Serra.

He turns and heads for a new patch of forest in the opposite direction.

Dusk turns to night. He wanders into the wood half awake, dizzy from hunger and exhaustion. The sounds of the day dim down and begin to meet the rising sounds of the night. Daytime birdcalls are replaced by the screech of owls and the rustle of creatures in the blackening undergrowth. The flap of moth wings replaces the buzz of flies and bees and butterflies. No rabbits, squirrels, blackbirds can be heard. Fresh noises come from bush, grass, marsh and treetop. Maklan's nerves become tense, tight like the string of a bow. Even the sound of his own feet breaking dry twigs makes him jagged and tetchy. Images rise and fall in his head, some so vivid they could be right in front of him in the twilight: Serra emerging from the river; the shadow boy on the edge of the forest; the hollow, cold eyes of the boy tribe across the flames of the fire; the wolfhound; Jacob, his worn wrinkled skin and piercing grey eyes. A dark object flies swiftly and silently past his head, then another. His mind rushes to figure out what they are. His fear gets the better of him and he runs. He looks for the last light of the day, the light that will get him back out onto the moor. He staggers, trips on a heap of small moss-covered rocks, and stumbles. He reaches out, catches hold of a tree just before he hits the ground. He stands, trying to catch his breath, feeling sick. He hears a sound from a low-lying thicket, a scurrying, startled movement; an animal, a big one, big enough to eat. He crouches down, trying to silence his breath. A mangy old badger emerges, sniffing the air. Maklan backs off; he knows the danger of badgers. If they get their teeth into you, their jaws lock and the only way to get them off is to kill them, cut their head off and cut and break their jaws apart piece by piece. The startled, grey-black animal looks around. It senses Maklan, looks straight at him, sizes him up, snorts and moves on. Maklan breathes relief. He is about to walk on when he hears more movement. He looks ahead. In the distance he sees the outline of a deer. He stands stock-still. A deer's eyesight isn't good but its animal sense is. If Maklan looks straight at it, it will feel his eyes on him. He looks at it out of the corner of his eye. It doesn't move. Maklan feels his knees beginning to tremble. He moves one step back. He doesn't feel it, the small twig underfoot, until it cracks. The deer springs from where it stands and sprints through the wood. Maklan has no choice but to chase it. The light is almost gone, only the openings in the tops of the trees giving any sense of the boulders and trees in his path. He takes out his blade from his leg binding and runs as fast as his legs will carry him. He jumps over boulders, dodges trees and shrubs, trying to keep pace with the fast-moving animal. He sees and senses its panic. He breathes deep, filling his lungs with air to give him more power. His adrenaline gives him more speed. His legs feel stronger. The deer gains ground, moving swiftly and easily through the half-lit wood heading for the light at the edge and open moor. If it reaches it, the deer and his meal will be lost. The thickening of the wood, trees, boulders and low-lying scrub and shrub are on his side, slowing the animal down enough for him to gain ground. He picks up more speed, pushing himself as hard as he can. He jumps onto a boulder, then another. He passes a stream. The dampness in the air makes the moss on the rocks slippery and wet. He lands, slips and slides down off a huge boulder and tumbles to the ground. He picks himself up and pushes himself forward and starts running again. He gets a few yards further when his shoulder clips the hard, gnarly bark of a massive oak. The impact spins him round. His vision blurs. The sting of the wound is quick and sharp. He knows blood will quickly follow. He gets up and begins sprinting again, desperately trying to get to the deer before it gets to the moor. The dusk light from the outside edge of the wood brightens as the trees and shrub begin to thin. Maklan's heart sinks. Almost suffocating from lack of air he stops, rests his hands on his knees and lets his chin drop to his chest.

The first thump doesn't get his attention. The second makes him look up. He holds his breath again. There is no sign of the deer. He begins to walk slowly and nervously toward the edge of the wood, to the source of the sound. The object on the ground slowly comes into focus. The panting, panicking deer lies at the base of a tree, eyes wide in terror. Maklan looks up at the bark and sees strands of deer hair... and blood. It has done something he has never known a deer to do. It has run into a tree and knocked itself to the ground. He kneels down and brings his hand to its back and feels the heat of its body, the rise and fall of its chest as it tries to catch its breath. Blood runs from its nose. Its belly is big, like it's eaten too much. But Maklan quickly realise that the swelling is not from food. His heart sinks. She has a fawn inside her. He didn't realise he'd been hunting a doe with fawn. The unwritten law of the hunter... never to kill doe with fawn. Her offspring will be food for the next season. He is filled with dread. He knows killing this way is always bad, the worst kind of omen. A man from his village tracked and killed a doe with fawn when Maklan was seven summers old. Within two days the hunter was dead from fever. Maklan backs away. The animal begins to cry out in blood-choked pain. He wants to leave her and run back into the wood. Pretend it never happened. But pity takes hold of him. He looks down at the animal and knows what he has to do. He takes a deep breath, kneels down and brings his blade to her neck.

'Forgive me, spirit of the forest.' He covers her eyes and pushes the blade through the hair, the skin and finally the flesh. Blood covers the shank of the metal, the handle and his hand in a thick, spilling, crimson mass. Within a few seconds the animal stops moving, a few seconds more and its breathing stops. He knows that now the animal is dead he must take what he needs for himself and move. Wolves will finish what's left of her. He begins to cut into her left hind leg. The severing takes longer than he expects, his blade is not nearly sharp enough. He rips the flesh with his hands, yanks and pulls the ball of bone out of the socket holding the leg to its body. He levers it, using his full body weight to pull back and tear it free. It takes all of his remaining strength. It finally rips and comes free and he stumbles back to the forest floor, breathing hard, feeling even more sick. His arms and legs are stained with the deer's dark, steaming blood. He must cleanse himself of it, eat the meat, keep the wolves away. He gets to his feet, taking one last look at the animal. He says a prayer of thanks. His fear of omen is shifted by a sense of pride at a good kill. He did his best. If he'd known she was with fawn, he would've stopped the chase in a heartbeat. But now at least he can eat.

He walks a hundred yards back into the wood, the weight of the hind leg getting heavier by the step. As he gets to the open space, something stops him dead in his tracks. A bad feeling in his gut, more fear.

He feels he's being watched from behind. He is tired of the fear.

'Must be one of the Lost Boy Tribe… or all of them?' He whispers to himself.

He keeps walking. Gut feeling becomes reality as he hears the footfall of more than two legs some way back. He walks on for a few more yards, head spinning, no idea what to do next.

He turns to see the animal cantering straight for him 'Oh Thunor, no.' He breaks into a sprint, the weight of the fresh meat immediately slowing him down. He shoots another quick look behind and sees the shadow of the animal as it thunders after him. He remembers the dream, Sanfar. The hammer of the animals hooves on the earth rage toward him. He pisses himself in terror. Despite the massive spread and weight of its antlers, the stag has no problem catching him up.

He feels and hears the rhythm of animal breath…

animal rage…

… the hard grunt of exhalation as each hoof hits the ground with increased force.

Hot, angry breath on the back of Maklan's neck.

Impact. Contact of antler on flesh.

Pressure, deep, hard, sharp, pushing into Maklan's back, forced by the weight and speed of the animal's unstoppable chase…

Split of skin and flesh.

Antler bone going in...

Pain.

Searing, biting, cutting, annihilating...

... pain.

The force of the huge animal on Maklan's back knocks the wind clean out of his lungs – ten times heavier, forcing him aggressively to the ground in a single paralysing hammer blow. Maklan feels more dirt in his mouth. Although terrified, he's also enraged at being attacked again. He clumsily turns his body face up, bringing his arms up to protect himself, pitifully holding his shaking, bloodied blade at the animal. The stag towers over him, draws its foreleg back into the ground several times, steam jetting from its nose, shaking its head from left to right, raging down at him. Everything slows for Maklan. He wishes he were back home. Wishes he had never come to this wood, never left Jacob Hill's hut, wishes he were with Serra, wishes Sanfar was with him now. His wishes amount to nothing. The wild animal rears up on its hind legs, pulls head and antlers back and slams its full body weight down. Maklan turns to protect himself. Antlers crash into his shoulders and back. His face is rammed so deep into the earth once more, forced onto the root of a tree. Both eyes are cut by the ancient wood. The pain so powerful he instantly loses consciousness. And in the blackness of quick, violent sleep, Jacob's words enter the wounded, deathly dreaming...

'Before the night is out, you will know the true meaning of blindness.'

Chapter Nineteen

VILLAGE OF THE
RIVER TRIBE

Where is everyone? I'm getting tired of looking at the inside of this old hut, these walls, the floor, the tiny candle and this old bed. I'm always waiting for mother and my next meal.

Where is she?

She just left, Serra. She's busy looking after our house, cooking your next meal.

I want her here...

She'll be back soon. So will father and Lorkan.

I can't stop thinking about him... Maklan. I have a bad feeling... that he's not alright. Maybe something has happened? I should go back to Jacob's place... to see what's happening, to see if he's alright.

I'm losing my mind.

I'm going out, I need to get some air, walk, stretch my legs.

Someone's coming.

'Serra? You in here? Thunor, it's so dark in here. You need some light. That candle's not enough.'

'Rasra?'

'Who do you think it is, sister?'

'Come and sit with me. Talk to me, tell me what's happening out there.'

'The usual. How are you?'

'My legs still ache, my whole body's hurting and I'm hungry.' *She looks like she wants to say something.* 'What is it, Ras?'

'Are you ready to tell me yet...?'

'Tell you what?' *Just tell her.*

'What happened to you out there? The whole village is arguing about what to do and they don't even know what happened. One of the crones said you'd been violated. Said she knew a violated sister when she saw one. There's a group of young warriors sitting round the fire with spears and blades and axes sharpened. They're ready to leave the village... just waiting to hear what the council decide.'

'They're in council?'

'Since you came back. Talking, talking, talking and none of them even knows what happened to you. Stupid way to go about it if you ask me. They even asked your family not to talk to you about it.'

'It is so good to have you here.'

'It's good to be here, to see you. Are you going to tell me what happened?'

'Have they sent you here to find out?'

'No, Serra. I'm not even meant to be here. They said no one's to talk to you till they do. I was worried about you. I knew something bad had happened.'

'It did.'

'Were you... violated?'

'Too many times to count.'

'What?!'

'I was tricked and captured by a group of young warriors a few days' walk from here. They took me back to their horrible village and kept me in a hut tied up for days and did what they wanted with me and left me there when they were done.' *She's not saying anything. Just staring at me with her mouth hanging open.* 'For Thunor's sake, say something, Ras.'

'I... don't know... what in Thunor's name am I supposed to say to that? There's nothing to say to make it better... to change it. But I do know what we do.'

'What?'

'We go to war. I'll tell the warriors round the fire and we go, today. No point waiting for the stupid elders to council this for the next three days. Sooner we get to them the better.'

'I can't go against what father wants. Mother said he wants me to wait.'

'If you leave it... if we wait, they could go, they could get away and then maybe we spend days or weeks hunting them down.'

'They're not going anywhere.'

'How do you know that?'

'Trust me. We'll go and see what they say once I've told tell them what happened. I'm not worried about their ruling, it's father's voice I trust and will follow. Have you seen Lorkan?'

'He's one of the ones sitting round the fire waiting. He is angrier than all of them put together.'

'Come. Let's get some air in our lungs and light on our bodies. I need to move my legs.'

'I'm right by your side, Serra, you know that.'

'Thank you, sister. I have missed you more than you know.' *Tell her about Maklan.*

In time. Let's do this first, then maybe I can find him, maybe bring him here... everyone can meet him.

Chapter Twenty

DEATH SENTENCE

Maklan opens his eyes but sees nothing. The pain vibrates throughout his body like blades and axes crashing into each other over and over, grinding and screaming. He wonders if he is dead or dying.

He sees nothing but black. He smells the forest floor, the morning air, it makes him feel like throwing up. He finds it close to impossible to get up. He pushes himself slowly up on his elbows but falls back down.

'Thunor, please... help me!!'

Birds in the treetops scatter. Only the wind fills his ears. He begins to retch. His empty belly rejects nothing except air and throat-burning bile.

His eyelids are tight shut. He brings his fingers to them. Thick, scabbed blood has set hard around them and most of his face. He feels a sudden rush of fear. He remembers where he is and wonders if the stag is still near. He tries to spit into his hand. No spit comes, his mouth dry and rank. He sucks what spit he can find from the inside of his cheeks, spits it out and dabs it gently onto his eyes. It makes little difference. He gropes around on the ground. His fingers find what he knows is a small clump of damp, soft moss. He rips it up from the solid, cold boulder and brings it to his eyes.

'Ahh, yes...'

After several minutes the scabs begin to soften around his eyes. He lies on his back and tries to come to terms with the pain.

After an hour on his back he removes the moss and feels around the wound. The thick, bloodied scab is loose enough, soft enough to remove. He gently brings his fingers to it and slowly pulls it away. The pain of it almost makes him pass out again. The scab peels away and his eyelids slowly open. There is excitement at the chance of being able to see. The lids quickly close to soothe the pain. After a few minutes he opens them again, waiting for daylight.

Nothing.

He is met only with blackness.

Both eyes... blinded.

He is starving.

He knows this is a death sentence in the wild.

'Please, get me back home. Had enough of this.'

He lifts himself, gets onto his knees and begins to crawl around, feeling his way, looking for the raw meat of his kill. He smells it first, then hears the humming buzz of what sounds like a swarm of flies. He crawls to the smell and the sound, fumbles around until his fingers find it. He swipes the flies away, picks up the doe leg. The wolves have been. The meat has been stripped to the bone. He thanks Thunor they didn't feed on him. He tries to find some flesh with his teeth. It makes him retch again. He but he holds down the bile, chewing on the meat a few times, brushing flies away from his mouth. He gives up hope of mashing it up into a digestible pulp and swallows the raw meat whole. He slumps onto his back. He feels the thick moss around and under him.

It brings little comfort. Exhausted, his eyes droop. He drifts into some kind of broken sleep. As he moves from waking to sleeping, images appear clear in his mind, as if he could see them in front of him, as if he weren't really blind: the shadow boy on the edge of the Lost Boy wood, the tribe fire, being handed the blindfold.

He remembers. He didn't give it back.

He reaches into his pocket and pulls it out. He rips up another clump of moss, puts it over his eyes and gently ties the bandage over the moss and around the back of his head. The wetness and pressure is soothing but the pain remains strong.

He tears up more moss and does all he can to suck the moisture from it.

'Got to get home... or die out here.'

CHAPTER TWENTY ONE

ANIMAL TRACKING

Jacob Hill moves through the forest at a steady pace, his footfall silent on the forest floor. His legs strong and connected to the earth. He is part of the wood, the land, the river. He knows the places to hunt; how to track any animal he chooses, one night rabbit, another pigeon, another wild boar. He has been walking for the best part of a day. His gut told him when it was time to leave. He set out with his wolfhound, food, herbal medicine, remedies and a rope. He has taken enough food for two days, for two people. The rest he will hunt.

He moves with confidence through the thick wood, over river, marshland, meadows and forest. His dog stays two feet behind at all times, silent and alert.

———

He finds Maklan long before Maklan has any idea he is anywhere near.

He stops and watches the boy stumble, half crouched in defensive alert, through the woodland, creeping his way forward using his dirt-blackened fingers as a guide. Jacob can see Maklan has been badly injured, his eyes covered with a makeshift bandage.

He has discovered true blindness.

He pities him but does not call out to him or go to him. He watches the blind boy work his way clumsily, slowly forward. He moves in the direction of the open moor, to the south, further from civilisation, further from the north, further from his tribe. Maklan is utterly lost; his staggering and stumbling taking him far from his path home. Jacob moves closer, keeping downwind. He silently commands his dog to lie and wait.

He gets close enough to Maklan to see the bandage and moss on his twisted, scarred face, the cuts, scratches, blood-stained shirt. He knows he will not make it far without help.

Maklan crawls on. Jacob and dog follow... some way behind.

Jacob follows Maklan for the next two hours until Maklan finally reaches a river. He sinks to the earth exhausted. After a few moments he crawls forward, drinking his fill of the river's clean, fresh water. Jacob watches him as he tentatively removes his bandage and rests his head back on a moss-covered rock. The hot afternoon sun shines multiple rays through the new leaves of the trees, warming his battered face. He falls quickly to sleep, dropping the bandage and moss to the ground.

Jacob waits until Maklan is deep in sleep before he approaches.

He moves like a gentle wind over the ground, little or no sound coming from him. He crouches silently beside Maklan, picks up the moss bandage and retreats a few yards. He takes out three healing herbs from his pack, rolls and crushes them deep into the moss, then brings the moss back to its original place and retreats.

Maklan wakes some time later and feels around for the bandage. He ties it back over his eyes, unaware of the medicine in the moss.

He gets to his knees, crawls back to the river and drinks more water. He stands, steadies himself and begins to walk back in the direction he came. He looks disorientated. He stops, confused, then walks left, in a new direction. He stops again then crouches down, bringing his hand to his forehead in despair.

Jacob knows it is time. He removes the rope from his bag, swings it in a wide circle and hurls it over to Maklan. It lands with a gentle thump at his feet. Maklan jumps with fright, looking around.

'Who's there?!?' Maklan shouts, alarmed and angry.

Jacob doesn't respond. Maklan rises to his feet in a defensive pose, blade in hand. He stands for a moment then takes a hesitant step back. He treads on the knot of the rope and stops. He leans down and feels for it. As he picks it up, Jacob unravels the long line from his bag. Maklan grips the rope.

'I've a blade and I'll cut any comes near me!!'

No reply.

Maklan holds the rope and gently pulls on it; it tightens. He looks blindly down at it, confused.

'What is this, some kind of sick Lost Boy trick?'

No reply.

Maklan stands, dumbstruck, unmoving, thinking, angry, confused.

Finally after many minutes, sensing no immediate danger, he realises he has nothing to lose. He feels his way slowly along the rope, cautious, agitated, but he follows it. He shakes his head and takes a firmer hold on the rope. The slack is pulled a little tighter. He feels himself being gently pulled... guided. He takes up the slack.

'Who's there?'

No answer.

Maklan begins to walk, slowly at first. He is aware he is being led in the opposite direction to the one he was traveling but it feels right.

'Speak to me. Where are you taking me?'

The rope tugs gently. It reassures Maklan; the simple movement encourages him to keep walking. There is no threat. He listens to his gut. He moves forward slowly, hunched and alert in case he walks into a tree or boulder. The pain in his eyes eases for the first time. There is a change in the direction of the wind. He feels a sense of hope inside his blindness. He wants now more than anything to be back with his tribe. And he wants to know who is guiding him.

He whispers to himself under his breath. 'Whoever you are, spirit or human... take me away from here, out of this wood.'

As he continues on he thinks of his father. Why he left the village. He wants to go back.

And he doesn't.

———

Maklan's father Baylan drank all day and night and did little or no work. He left the gathering of herbs, root vegetables and berries to his wife and the hunting to his eldest son, Tenmar. Baylan told Maklan he was ashamed to have a son who could not bring the meat of deer or salmon home to the table yet. Maklan knows how to snare rabbit, fox and otter, but he has not been shown how to hunt and take down the bigger animals, boar, deer and stag, by Baylan who still expects him to be able to do it, like it is something natural. Baylan refused to teach him how and beat him for not knowing. Maklan was confused and angry at the man who was meant to love him and teach him the ways of the forest and river as other fathers did. He watched and secretly followed other fathers as they took their sons to the moor and river, tracked them silently, unseen for hours, trying to learn the ways of the hunter for himself. He longed for a father who would do the same. His brother Tenmar taught him all he knew but it wasn't enough, not for Baylan.

And now Maklan has killed a doe with fawn. His first kill, marked with bad omen. And he is blinded for his trouble.

I blame you for this, father. If you'd taught me, I wouldn't be in this storm of trouble, blind, wounded. Finished.

His thoughts move back to the last time he saw his father. The time he promised himself would be the last day he laid eyes on the man who gave him life. That day in his village was hot. The air heavy with flies and insects covering the shithouse by the boundary-line fence. Maklan had been sent to earth it over by his father; the job he hated most. Baylan was standing over him swaying to the rhythm of the alcohol in his blood, sneering at Maklan.

'You good for nothing… dung-for-brains fool boy. You're an embarrassment thass wot you are! Can't even shovel shit proper. Look at you; no son of mine would agree to shovel that muck without a fight. You've no shpine. You're a girl-boy, thass your problem isn't it? Thass what's up with you, no shpine in your scrawny, useless little girl-boy body.'

Baylan had been taunting Maklan all morning. Maklan hummed silently to himself to block out the drunken words. It worked to begin with. But the slurred voice of the man he hated more than anything in the world finally started to grind him down, eat into him like a rusty saw blade until finally… he snapped. He filled the shovel to the hilt with human and animal shit. He looked down at it, building up courage, getting ready to do what he knew would change everything.

'Wassamatter, loss the strength in those puny good for nothin' girl-boy arms avya? A little human turd too much for ya, is it?!'

Maklan looked at him sidelong, then lifted the heavy shovel with ease up to head height.

'Oooh, big man *can* lift a little turd… been eatin' ya vittles, eh son? Thass ma boy!' Baylan's left shoulder drooped down and he sneered sideways at his son. 'So you're the big man of the village now, are ya, boy? Big man with big plans, eh? What ya doin' with that then, eh? Take it to the elder hut as an offerin'? All they're good for, might as well.'

Maklan walked over to him, slowly. Baylan stopped swaying and looked directly at him. 'Wass up, need some help? Shure... I'll give you some help... we can lay it at their door as a little pressie. Father an son doin' their bit for the community. Good lad. Good lad.'

Maklan slowly swung the shovel behind him and readied himself. It was then his father realised what was about to happen. His face shifted from a twisted snarl to jaw-dropped surprise. Maklan swung the shovel round. And the dung came flying off. A shovel-load of shit smacked into his father's bleary-eyed face, covering him from head to toe.

The village stopped dead, as if holding its breath, waiting for what they knew would come. The familiar rage, the beating of the boy too young to defend himself.

What happened to break the silence wasn't what anyone was expecting. Baylan looked around, dazed, confused, blinking through thick brown muck for a long, slow moment, then he did something Maklan would never forget. Something he never expected. His father brought his hands up to his face, dropped to his knees and started to wail like a beaten dog. The silence of the villagers deepened until a small child pointed at the big man covered head to toe in shit and started giggling, then cackling, then laughing. The laughter carried through the village. One by one, man, woman and child began pointing and crying with tears of laughter at the drunken mess of a man, howling into his hands, a growing black swarm of flies buzzing round him. He kept his hands firmly over his face as if he could actually hide from what was happening. Then, as suddenly as he had started howling, he stopped. He rose unsteadily to his feet walked over to Maklan, took the shovel from his son's shaking hand, looked at it for a moment, feeling its weight, then hit Maklan hard across the side of the head. Maklan saw white stars then black, then dropped to the ground. The village fell into shocked silence. Blood crept from the side of his head. Barely conscious, he held the wound, looked at his bloodstained hand then back up at his father, tears streaming down his face thinning the thick, dark blood.

That's when everything changed for Maklan. He'd had enough. He rose to his feet, drew his skinning knife from his leg binding and slashed the pitiful mess of a man that was his father across his shit-covered cheek. Three clean cuts on cheeks and nose. Then he wiped the blade on his shirt, put it back in his leg binding and walked away from the village swearing never to go back.

Chapter Twenty Two

HOME-FIRE BURNING

I know this place, know it like the back of my hand. Could walk it blind.

You are blind, Maklan.

Can feel the sun rising, the heat of it, warming up my bones. Everything smells familiar. The earth, river, trees, wood-smoke, the sounds. Food... cooking... broth... meat. Young ones playing. Familiar voices. Becoming clearer. I know these voices.

Please let this be it; please, Thunor, let this be my village.

You said you never wanted to come back. Make your mind up.

That was then. I wasn't blind then.

Rope still guiding me. Taking me closer to the sounds.

Closer.

Closer.

This place feels very familiar. Feels right.

Rope's slackening...

Voices. I know those voices! That's Sanfar's little brother and his sister Freya!!

You're home, Maklan. This IS your village!

'Tenmar! COME OPEN THE GATE, BROTHER, IT'S MAKLAN, I'M BACK!!! I need your help... and I need something to eat...'

Someone's here, right next to me. Touching my hand. Small hand, a child's hand? Squeezing my fingers, leading me in. 'Who's there?' *Leading me in through the gates. Voices stopping, the children playing, stopping.*

They've seen me. Coming toward me.

'What's happened to his eyes, mother?'

I can feel them around me. Looking at me. Feels familiar, not sure I like it. Had this with the Lost Boys. Doesn't feel so threatening. More like they're curious.

'Look at him. Looks like he's been in a fight. Nasty one too, looks of those cuts and bruises. Wonder what the other one looks like?'

Laughing. They laughing at me? Sick of people thinking I'm some kind of fool.

Relax. This isn't the Lost Boy Tribe.

'Just like his father. I said he'd come back in the end, didn't I? Eh? Said he'd come running home to his mother.'

Lot of people here. Can feel them, coming closer. Looking at me like I'm some kind of wild animal.

'Where have his eyes gone, mother?'

Can't see them, but I can feel them.

'Don't look at him, child.'

'Someone help him. He looks weak.'

Must be the whole village here.

'Get him some food... and water. Bring him to the fire.'

I should leave the village and get attacked by wild animals more often. Never had a greeting like this before.

'Tell the elders Maklan is back and he's wounded.'

This little hand, still holding me, leading me to the fire... so soft, gentle. Can feel the warmth of the skin, the heat of the fire getting closer, smell of food getting stronger.

'Maklan! Please, let me through. Thank Thunor! You're home... where have you been!?'

'Mother? Is that you?'

'He's gone all shaky. Look at his legs. Looks like he's going to fall.'

'Someone catch him before he does himself an injury!'

Yes... please... someone...

... catch me.

CHAPTER TWENTY THREE

RIVER TRIBE ELDERS

It feels good to be back within the village walls. Feeling the hard earth under my feet again. My legs still feel weak though. I've been lying down too long. Why isn't Rasra saying anything? She never normally stops talking... and why's she walking behind me? 'Walk beside me, Ras. Why are you so quiet?'

'I don't want them to see me talking to you. You know what they're like, always wanting the last word.'

'Do we have to go in there? It's so warm out here. I'd prefer to stay out here in the light and the heat and the sun. What do they want to do?'

'More of their stupid rituals. Been doing them since before the dawn of time, blah blah blah. Just tell them what happened and be done with it. Then we can get on with what needs to be done, track down and deal with the ones who took you from us.'

'What if they don't let me go? What if they don't even send a search party?'

'And when was the last time what the elders said ever stopped you doing what you wanted to do, Serra of the River Tribe?'

She's right. We need to just get this over with. I'll tell them what happened, then we can get there and do what needs to be done. 'Stay near, Ras. I need you close.'

'I'm not letting you out of my sight again in a hurry.'

Here it is, the hut. I've never been inside before. I've never wanted to.

Here goes.

Take a deep breath.

I can feel Ras close behind. It feels safer with her here.

Who was that standing at the door? I didn't recognise her. All the old ones look the same to me.

I can't see a thing. It's so smoky in here, there's no daylight.

Wait for your eyes to get used to it... to the dark. It smells of old people and sweat and smoke and sage.

'Welcome Serra. Sit down, sister.'

That's the one who was at my first bleed. She scared the life out of me.

Lorkan! Thank Thunor. Wave him hello...

He's watching me like a hawk. As always. He looks so serious.

Everyone is looking at me. Like they're waiting for me to say something. All the elders are here, men, women, everyone has come.

The old scary one... she looks like she's about to say something.

'We are all deeply saddened and angered by the news of a child of our village being attacked while on her first lone hunting trip. We need to know what happened to you out there.'

'I was hurt.' *I can't look her in the eye. It makes me feel like crying.*

'Go on...'

Here is no place to cry. Just tell them what happened, Serra. 'There was a man... a boy. He wasn't part of the village. He was in the hut with me... where they held me... he helped me escape. I'd be dead without him.'

'And...?'

'He should be rewarded... given something.'

'That is up to you. This is not what we are here to discuss. We want to know what happened to you. Who helped you escape can come later.'

'I was... I...'

'Take your time, sister.'

'I was attacked by a group of men... boys. I think it was four sunrises ago. I met a boy on the edge of the village who I thought was safe, thought could be trusted... I liked him. So I walked with him, across our river. He tricked me and trapped me. He took... I tried to fight them off... but there were too many of them. They came from everywhere... they took me by surprise. I fought them off as long as I could but there were too many of them.'

Close your eyes and keep breathing. 'I was taken to their village, two days' walk from here. They made me a prisoner and they... they violated me... day and night. They never took the ropes from my ankles.' *Everyone is looking at me. Staring into me. I can see their eyes in the dark, like they're wondering if I'm telling the truth.*

'Who were these boys... where were they from?'

'None of them were from around here, except the one I thought I could trust. He said he was from the Forest Tribe.' *I don't want to do this.*

Breathe, Serra. 'I want to go on a search party and bring them back here... I don't want them wounded or hurt. Wounds fade, shame lasts. I want them to be ashamed of what they've done to me and for everyone to see that.' *Why is the old crow shaking her head?*

'You will not be able to go with any party that we may send from here. No woman can join this kind of search party, that is village law, you know that. You are too close to this. Even if we let you go, your anger and pain will cloud your ability to think clearly. We need to decide what we are to do. You will return to your hut and we will let you know what decision we have come to when we come to it.'

'I'm staying. I have a right to stay... to see what you decide to do about what has happened to me. This happened to me not you, and I want to be here.' *Lorkan's coming over. He's going to try and take me out of the hut.* 'Leave me alone, Lorkan. I'm staying. I have a right to stay!'

'Come, Serra, you have to leave. I'll take you back to our hut. We can talk.'

'I don't want to talk! I want to stay. I've been violated, beaten and battered and had to find my own way home. I'm staying. No one is going to take me out of this hut until I know what's to be done.'

Lorkan is smiling at me, like he's sorry, like he understands. He does. I know he does. He knows I'm right. He'll stay here with me. And he will come with me; so will Rasra, soon as we're out of here and away from stupid tribe law. I need my tribe-sister and my brother in here with me... and out there. I can't do this alone... I can't sit in here while some dried-up leathery old crones who've never gone through what I went through make up their minds what to do.

She's thinking, scratching her hairy chin. I'll listen, but I'm not shifting. I'm not leaving. Lorkan knows that. That's why he's sitting down next to me, his leg touching mine. Letting me know he's with me. He'll do anything to protect me. That's why the old crone is looking at me like that. Because she knows too. She's secretly on my side. She scares me but she's on my side.

She's standing up.

She's going to say something.

'Let Serra stay.'

CHAPTER TWENTY FOUR

TRICKED AND TRAPPED

Last Half Moon

Serra had not seen the young man on the edge of the village before. But he caught her eye immediately. He came to her, smiling, with a bunched handful of borage and sage, holding them out in front of him as a gift.

'I've been watching you for a while,' he told her. 'But I've only just found the courage up to talk to you. You seem a bit fierce.' He smiled when he said the word fierce.

'What do you want?' Serra asked defensively.

'I want to give you these.' He handed her the flowers. 'And I want to take you for a walk.'

'Why would I go on a walk with you? I've never seen you before. Do you think a bunch of flowers is enough to buy a walk with me?' She liked him.

'Because of the way you're looking at me now.'

'I'm not looking at you in any way.'

'And now you're going red in the face so I know you want to come on a walk with me.'

'You really think you're something special, don't you?'

'Yes.'

'Well, you aren't, not to me.'

'Why don't you come with me and you can make your mind up properly; give me some time to prove how special I am before you cast me off like a piece of bad rabbit.'

Serra waited a while, taking her time, keeping her eyes on him, checking him out, trying to unnerve him. He just looked straight back at her, calm and easy. 'If you come back tomorrow, same time, no flowers, I'll let you know if I want to walk with you or not. Now go, before my brother sees you and comes and scalps your cocky little head.'

She watched him walk away. Just as he reached the brow of the hill he turned to look back. She ducked down out of sight before he fully turned round. She put her head above the tall grass to watch this tall, handsome warrior disappear back over the brow of the hill.

———

She went back the next day, same time, same place and he was waiting for her. No flowers.

'You came.' He said with a smug smile on his face. 'Knew you would.'

She used her spirit sense on him and it told her she could walk with him.

'I'll walk with you for an hour, no more. And you will have to keep your hands to yourself. And stop staring at me like that. I don't like it.'

She walked with him when she knew she shouldn't, not without her father's permission and mother's blessing. She told the village she was going hunting. She was bewitched by the young man and his chiseled, sharp looks, his strong body, his eyes and the attention they gave her. She forgot the words of the elders. He told her he was a leader of men, a hunter. She thought he looked too young to be a leader but she believed he could hunt. He had the body for it. Lean muscles, long legs, a wiry look.

They walked beyond Strider's Ridge, through woods and across rivers, talking sweetly of the slow shift in season, of each other's village life, prey they had lost and won. She felt easy in his company, she felt good around him. They crossed the mighty Oak River. The river of her tribe. She had never passed it before. It took them some time to get across. The young hunter helped her, boulder to boulder. When she lost her balance between river and stone he held her hand, firm but gentle. She felt safe in his hands. They finally reached the other side.

That was when she noticed it. Like a spell had been lifted. The other side of the water felt full of danger. The young hunter, still holding her hand, began to clench it tighter, not out of the affection she had felt while crossing the river but now out of force. Something had changed in him. She felt darkly threatened. She wanted to be back on the other side. She didn't show him the panic she had rising inside. She needed to think fast. He force-led her into the wood, away from the river and escape.

Something was hidden in the trees up ahead. The hunter in her sensed it. Not animals, or wind or bird. This was human. Humans. Well concealed now but she knew they were there. She could easily read the signs of their presence in the shoulder-height broken branches, the tall grass trodden down by many sandalled feet, the spring bracken flattened. No animal would do that much damage simply moving through the forest. Only human hunters would be so careless because they know that animals do not read the visual signs. They depend on smell and sight. And none of these hidden humans reckoned on Serra being able to read their presence so easily, so quickly. But by the time Serra had spotted the signs, it was too late. The young hunter held her hand tighter.

'What are you doing?! Let my hand go! I don't want to be here. I trusted you! I'm going back to the other side and I don't need your help.' Serra pulled, trying to get her hand free, but couldn't.

'You're not going anywhere but back to our village.'

'What village? ' Serra tried again to pull her hand free but it was gripped and crushed tight in his wide, powerful hand. 'Let go of me or I'll cut you from ear to ear!'

He shook his head and tutted. 'I don't think that's how this is going to unfold.' He raised his fingers to his lips and gave a low whistle. The young warriors began to emerge from behind trees and bushes and from the undergrowth, silent as the earth, eyes focused on Serra, moving forward toward her. Some were covered in bracken camouflage, some had painted their faces with black and brown earth. They rose like the living dead from their hiding places and began to move slowly toward Serra. She opened her lips to scream but the young hunter pulled her violently toward him, covering her mouth with his hand before she could get a sound out. The first boy to reach her had a pointed face, he leered at her as he came closer. He was followed by a shorter, fatter young man with blue woad-streaked body, spear in hand. Then another and another and another. Each staring hungrily at her, scanning the curves of her body, grinning like wolves. The young hunter wrapped one arm around her neck and the other round both her arms. She tried to scream again through her palm-covered mouth. Nothing but a muffled cry. She stamped down hard on his foot and he released her, hopping, shouting and cursing her. She managed to wriggle free, stumble, fall and pull out her dagger. She leaped up and swung it in a wide, threatening circle, fending them off as they approached. As one of them tried to grab for her she lurched forward, catching him on the arm. Blood flowed fast. She moved forward, teeth bared, hissing like a mountain cat, ready to take out the heart of any that came within blade strike. They backed off. She moved forward, full of terrified rage. One lunged at her. She jabbed him twice, quick, sharp in the stomach and he stumbled to the ground, crying like a baby, looking at his blood-stained hand then up at her with a confused, pitiful look on his dirt-streaked face. In anger, forgetting the rest, she bore down on him to finish him. Arms grabbed her from behind. She didn't know how many. Hands with weapons, clubbing her, scratching at her, tearing at her animal skin, her human skin; a confused tangle of force, ripping deerskins from her, stripping her naked. Her blade was knocked from her hand. She prayed for a quick death. Begged the spirits and ancestors not to let her suffer at these young, hungry hands. The final blow to the side of her head came from the boy whose arm she had cut. She felt her knees buckle and blackness rise quickly into her eyes. The last thing she saw was the gleam of lust and anger on the blue-streaked face of the stomach-stabbed boy.

Quick, violent sleep followed.

CHAPTER TWENTY FIVE

TENMAR

Where am I? Still can't see anything. Just bits of light coming in from different places. Someone's in here, sitting on the edge of the bed.

Check your eyes.

Feel better.

Bandage gone. Something else covering them, cloth, something soft and wet...

... feels good.

Get some air on them, some light.

Slowly.

'Herbs need time to work. You should wait.'

'Tenmar? How long you been there, bro? You been watching me in my sleep again?'

'Someone's been in here with you since you got here. Mother most of the time. You said some pretty wild things in your sleep.'

'Need some water. Mouth feels like a rat's arse.'

'Here.'

'Thank you.'

'Are you totally blind?'

'Blind enough that I don't have to see your ugly face.'

'What happened? You look like death warmed up.'

'Attacked by a stag. Chased me through the woods, slammed me down, spiked my eyes.'

'You did something to deserve it?'

'Need a piss.'

'Let me help.'

'The day I can't take myself for a piss... stick an arrow through me. How long have I been here? Feel so stiff can hardly move my legs!' *Air feels good on my face out here.*

'Two days. Watch where you're going, bro! Nearly walked into the hut!'

'Stop fussing. Come with me.'

'Elders want to see you.'

'What for? Sun's bright.'

'Thought you were blind?'

'I can see light... shapes. Think some of it's coming back, slowly. What the old ones want me for?'

'Didn't say. Sent me to come get you.'

'Yesss. Thunor that feels GOOD! Feels like I haven't pissed in days.'

'You haven't.'

'It's good to be back with you, brother. Good to be out of the woods. Home.'

'You too. Here.'

'What's this?'

'A stick... to get about with.'

'Don't need a stick. Know every inch of this stupid village like the back of my hand.'

'Stop being an idiot. Take it. Take the stick.'

'If it keeps you quiet.'

'Where you going, brother?'

'The elders' hut.'

'It's this way, you fool.'

'I knew that. Come on then, what you waiting for Tenmar?'

'You.'

———

Never been in here. Not properly. Not like this. Not since I was a youngster, not since I sneaked in that night and watched what they did with all their rituals and pipe smoking and drinking and chanting. Same smell in here... pipe weed. Weird coming in through the front opening, even weirder doing this blind.

'Hey! Watch what you're doing with that stick! You'll have someone's eye out with that.'

'Sorry. Sorry.' *Who's that? Someone's taking my arm.*

'It's me, brother.'

Tenmar. 'Thank you, brother.'

'Sit down here, Maklan.'

'Are you rested, Maklan?'

That's the chief. 'Yes. Thank you.'

'And well?'

'I feel better but I still can't see.'

'You have defied village law by leaving and for that you will be punished.'

Punished? And I haven't had enough of that already?

'You know your father has gone. Where he went I do not know nor have much care. When you have rested you will come back here and we will tell you what we have decided to do with you. Tenmar, take him back to your family hut and let him rest. Come to us when you think he is well enough to sit with us again.'

'Is that it?'

'Leave it, Maklan. Let's go, brother.'

'You asked me to come here to tell me that you will decide in time what you're going to do with me? I nearly lost my life. *Calm yourself, Maklan.* 'If it wasn't for...' *Who was it lead me back here?*

'If it wasn't for what, Maklan?'

I'd like to punch his smug-sounding face in. 'If it wasn't for the one who led me back here... I would be dead.'

'Come on, Maklan, it's time to go.'

'No wait, Tenmar, I'm not leaving.'

'Yes, we are.'

'Tenmar, let go my arm, brother.'

'We're going, before you get into any more trouble. Get up.'

CHAPTER TWENTY SIX

TURNIP BOY

Sanfar sits in the darkened room, hunched over the flickering candle stub, clay pipe in his mouth, eyes closed as he draws the thick white smoke of silverine into his lungs. He feels its solid warmth move down his throat and seep into his body, muscles, tendons, blood, and finally... his aching bones. He listens to the rumble of carts outside the solidly-built oak hut, the sounds of people arguing, singing, talking, buying, selling, footfall up and down the track. On and on it goes. He likes the rhythm of it but doesn't want to be in it. Relaxed by the silverine he allows himself to rest. Maklan flashes into his mind. If he wasn't so out of it he might miss his tribe-brother. He remembers the last time he saw him, the anger, watching him walk away through the trees into the distance. He'd stay angry with him if he could, but he can't... not for long. He leans forward and brings the candle flame to the blackened base of the clay pipe, waiting for the smoke to emerge. Memories of hunting with Maklan come back to him; crawling through bracken and thicket as children; tracking their first deer; rain pouring down hard, wind blowing, covering their scent;

neither of them noticing the cold, just the focus on the animal they would kill if they were big enough. The animal was faster and smarter than both of them put together.

Along with the fresh rush of silverine, the memory fills Sanfar with a little happiness. But this is quickly attacked by the memory of what he had to do to stop the ache in his bones and find some peace. The events of earlier that day flood his head with violence... too much for the silverine to block out.

He goes over and over it, cursing himself. He remembers Bones standing in the doorway, watching him as he headed down the well-worn dirt track, into the darkness, the rat-infested mud trying to suck the shoes off his feet. After almost an hour the sound of the streets, its chaos and noise faded away until all he could hear was his own footfall on the ground beneath him. He moved through the darkening of the day, muscles, tendons and bones screaming for silverine.

An hour further on to the rambling, ramshackle edge of Heartfall, he reached the small encampment that Bones had described to him. Cooking fires were burning outside two of the bigger huts, blue smoke rising into the night sky. Children played in the growing dark, women cooked round the larger of the two fires, talking among themselves. They didn't notice Sanfar as he slipped into the shadows behind the huts. He used his hunting skills to stay silent, unseen and unheard, even if his legs were shaking from the fear of getting caught. The earth was now soft beneath his feet. It began to squelch up between the gaps in the leather toes. He knew he had reached the area where the village shithouse was. The stench of human waste filling his nostrils made him gag. He kept moving.

He finally found the hut Bones had described at the far end of the village. There were voices inside, talking, serious and low. He waited ages for them to finish and for two men to leave the hut and head back into the centre of the village. He walked round the front and headed inside.

A man stood in front of him, tall, skinny, bone-white skin; the hollow look around his eyes made his face look like a living skull.

Sanfar walked into the middle of the hut. The two men stood facing each other, a look of recognition in their eyes.

'You know why I'm here...' Sanfar waited for a reply. The skinny man said nothing. He simply nodded.

'You have what Zed wants?'

No reply.

'Don't make me ask again.' Sanfar took out the blade, his palm sticky with the sweat of withdrawal from the silverine and the fear of the fight he knew was coming. 'You know what you owe and I'm here to collect.' Sanfar could easily see the man in front of him had the silverine withdrawal in his bones.

He shook his head. 'I have nothing. The men just left... took the last of it. No coin for your master, not today. Come back another day. I'm sick as a pig, I need some silverine, looks like you do too. Maybe we can work together... get some for the both of us.'

'Bones said you'd say that.' Sanfar showed him the blade. 'Just give me what's owed and I'll leave, no blood, no trouble. Up to you.'

Sanfar waited a long time for a response before he stepped forward. The skinny, skull-faced junky stepped back into the half-darkness at the back of the hut. He moved fast but Sanfar moved faster, jabbing the blade at him with his full body weight, forcing the blade into his skinny belly. He let out a gasp and a pitiful grunt. Sanfar let go of the blade and watched him fall away onto the floor. The sigh he let out as he hit the ground sounded like relief, eyes open, looking up at the space above him. Sanfar couldn't move. That wasn't meant to happen. The blade was just to scare him, get the coin, get the silverine. It wasn't his fault. Sanfar snapped out of his trance, removed his blade from the body and began searching through the fallen man's hut for the coin. It didn't take long to find the bag of coin hidden beneath his bed in a greasy black pouch. He took it all, crept out of the hut and headed back to Heartfall, not knowing if the man was dead or alive.

Sanfar is snapped out of the memory and the guilt by the sound of the hut door opening. Captain Bones walks in and looks down at Sanfar.

'Well, you had you a skinful of what you needed, ain't you, look at the state of you. Hey brothers, come look at this fool!'

Sanfar looks up, bleary eyed, half conscious as the doorway fills with the dirty, scarred faces of Zed's men, looking in, jeering down at him, the sound of their mocking voices muffled in his ears as if under water. They point and laugh and take the piss. One of them chucks a rotten turnip at him. It lands in his lap. He picks it up and looks at it as if it had fallen from the sky. He sniffs and takes a bite from it. The mass of faces laugh even louder.

'Zed has another collection for you, Turnip Boy. When you're straight enough to get up off your scrawny little arse.'

Sanfar shrugs his shoulders and carries on eating the turnip. Happy to forget the blade and the hut and the bleeding silverine junky.

CHAPTER TWENTY SEVEN

BAYLAN

Maklan's father walks through Heartfall, eyes down on the muddied, rubbish-filled road. He walks like so many of the other lost souls in the city, without looking where he's going. People coming toward him dodge him and curse him as they pass. A small boy follows him, pulling faces and chucking bits of dirt at him. He's pulled back by his mother and smacked round the head just as he's about to chuck a rock. Maklan's father walks like he has somewhere to go; he doesn't. He walks hoping that he will know where it is when he gets there. He doesn't know this town and he doesn't like it. The memory of his village is blurred by a skin-full of cheap, gut-rotting mead, his stomach aching from too much liquid and a lack of food. He hasn't eaten for three days.

He walks and walks. Day becomes night. He gets to know each corner of the town, its shops, streets, beggars, drunks, bone men pulling beaten-up carts with bodies piled high to be carried to the lime pits on the edge of the sprawling town. He picks up scraps of food from the back of taverns, butchers', bakers' and grocers' shops, takes water from cattle troughs, sleeps in door-ways, near stables and horses for heat on the cold clear nights. He wanders, his mind emptying of any hope, his heart cold, the same well-worn anger sitting like a rock in his belly. Chaotic thoughts spill out of his mind, through his lips into the mutterings of the madman everyone around him sees, hears and avoids. Passers-by no longer get close enough to dodge him. They see him way ahead and give him the widest possible berth, staring at him long and hard, waiting, fearing and wondering if he will attack them or lash out or shout at them as other madmen do. He keeps walk-ing with no destination in mind, day and night, through rain and sun, feeling more and more lost with each footfall. No one look-ing at him would imagine he had a past, a family, a village, a life. No one would imagine that he would have had a childhood, a time when he hunted the moors, alone, to get away from his vil-lage of birth, his own raging father who beat him by the light of the fire of the forge he grew up in, for no good reason other than he was drunk and short of work and coin. No one would imagine this raving man, with dead eyes and loose-hanging arms, wan-dering through this town of the dead, used to stay up through the night just to see the sun rise over the river and watch the thin yellow light of a new day hit the water and light up the forest and riverbanks and paths. No one here would believe this raving man would sit by fires with friends and talk through the night till the break of day about the day's hunting. No one in this town would know or care that this man left his village a young man with wide-eyed hope that he would find a new life on another part of the moor, a life free from fear. Find a village, work, a woman; make a family, live peacefully. No one would know how much courage it took to do this, how scared he was the night he left, silently, with a small pack on his back, swearing never to return. He kept his promise and has never been back. No one in this city would care how many nights he spent on the moors and rivers alone as he wandered on, searching, much like he wanders now. But back then when he was a lost boy he had hope and belief to keep him moving, to keep him heading south, away from his village of birth, away from fear and beatings to where the great Oak River was supposed to run wide and wild and be full to the brim with salmon. Where the weather was warmer, the rain softer and the winds less harsh. The boy who was to become Maklan's father moved further and further south until he reached the shoreline of the great ocean, where he stayed for three moons; catching food from the sea, lobsters, fish, feeding his skinny bones, making up for the starvation he'd had to deal with on his long journey. His hunting was in its early stages and he didn't know this new land or how to catch the animals he was used to catching. It seemed the animals down south knew he was a stranger and knew his tricks and traps avoiding them easily. After three moons this boy moved back inland, stronger, more confident of his hunting skills. He moved back into the forests, still searching for a place to call home, to rest his bones, a fire to sit by, new friends.

He searched until the leaves on the high, ancient oaks began to turn brown, until the winds from the north began to blow colder, to bite into his skin. One night, by the fire, sitting alone, eating a plump, spit-roasted rabbit, a young woman tracked him. She startled him but joined him and ate with him and stayed the night with him, by the fire. This young woman told him of her village and her kin and of the good hunting and that she'd take him there the following day. He accepted her offer with gratitude and slept better that night than any of the nights of the previous moons

Not a soul in this dark town would care of the endless days of spring he felt in the company of the young woman who would become his wife and bear him three strong children. The woman whose family would help him build a forge that men from all over England would hear of and come to for his craftsmanship. All this was ahead of him when he was a boy, when hope was strong. A hope slowly eaten by the ghosts of his childhood village... and his father. Ghosts that came to him at night, entered his dreams and tortured his thoughts, attacked him, robbed him of sleep and reason and drove him slowly to the mead huts of the new village and to violence with other drunken villagers; violence he eventually took to his own home, his wife and his children. He had sworn he would never do what his father had done, swore never to become his father, but over the years that's exactly what happened. No one in this town would know or care that this broken man wandering through their city streets had endured such a life. He blames his sons, Tenmar and Maklan for reminding him of who he once was. The hope he once had.

He stops in the middle of the street; people steer well clear of him. He looks up at the sky but sees nothing but the grey rain falling into his eyes, disguising fat tears rolling onto his cheeks.

'You look lost, brother.'

He hears the voice but ignores it.

'Look like you need something to warm your bones.'

Maklan's father brings his eyes back to street level and looks at the young man in front of him, pockmarked face, grinning, wanting something. 'That's me. The bone-warmer. Captain Bones, help you with what ails you, brother. You have coin?'

'I look like I have coin?'

'Not a problem. You're a big man, you do us a favour we'll give you what you need.'

Maklan's father feels a flicker of life behind his eyes, behind the anger. He reaches out his hand. 'Baylan. What kind of warmth you have in mind, brother?'

CHAPTER TWENTY EIGHT

DO NOTHING

How long is Nasa going to take saying what she's going to say?

Calm, Serra.

Something must be done. The old ones can help if they want to but they're wasting time.

Why is she looking at me like that? Like she's trying to understand what I'm thinking. Just tell me what you're going to do.

'Serra, we have decided.'

'Yes, Nasa?'

'Nothing will be done, not for now, not until we have the other villages with us.'

'But that could take days.' *Lorkan's coming over to me.*

'Serra... listen to what Nasa has to say, sister.'

'You're meant to be on my side, Lorkan.'

'I am. Just listen to what she has to say.'

'As elders we have given this much thought. This is a serious matter. You have been violated and these boys must be punished. We are not the only ones seeking vengeance for dishonour to tribe. There are two other tribes, both have had young women taken... We know there are many child warriors in that village and we need more men to defeat them. We will not risk our men being outnumbered, hurt or killed. We need to be sure we can win this battle.'

'You told me if I couldn't take care of myself my warrior brothers would.' *Don't start crying, Serra, not here.*

'We will send Lorkan to the two villages to gather a search party. This party will find the Lost Boy village and bring them back here where they will be properly punished.'

'Please. We should just go there, now. I know where the village is. I know what they look like, the ones who attacked me. We could be there in two days.'

'It has been decided. When Lorkan returns with the other men we will do what needs to be done.'

'Then I'll go with them. I can tell them which ones violated me.'

'You cannot leave this village. Not now. You will stay here and wait for their return.'

Chapter Twenty Nine

BLOOD-BROTHERS

What are you doing, Maklan?

Leaving.

Blind? You're leaving blind?

I'm not going alone. I'm taking him with me.

What if he doesn't come?

He will.

You should wait till you can get around without a stick.

I'm not waiting. Sanfar could die out there.

He won't die. He's quick and sharp.

He was. He's my tribe-brother and I'm going find him... with or without my eyes. 'Tenmar. Wake up brother! Come on, wake up!'

'Eh? Hey. Stop shaking me. What's going on? How come you're dressed? It's the middle of the night.'

'We're leaving. You and me. To go find Sanfar. You have to come with me. I need your eyes, brother.'

'Go back to sleep, you madman. I'm not going anywhere except back to my dreams of the chief's daughter.'

'I can't go out there on my own.'

'So don't. Go back to bed.'

'Then I'll go without you.'

'You'll get as far as the river if you're lucky and you'll probably fall into that. Your eyes need more time.'

'Anything could've happened to him!'

'Sanfar will be alright, you know that.'

'I've a bad feeling... something's happened.'

'You can't know that. Go back to sleep.'

'You promised.'

'Promised what?'

'You swore, that day by the river... when we drew blood together with our blades, the three of us. You swore you would do anything to protect me and Sanfar. We are sworn by oath of blood to protect each other.'

'That's dirty, brother. And it's not going to change my mind.'

'Would you be able to forgive yourself?'

'For what?'

'If something happened to him and we didn't at least try to get him back?'

'I can't believe you're doing this to me.'

'Come on, Tenmar. Come with me. We can hunt together, walk, talk about old times.'

'Don't much feel like hanging out with you right now, brother.'

'You coming?'

'You're unbelievable.'

'So you'll come?'

'Tomorrow. We'll go after dark. Three days. That's it... then I'm coming back. Now go back to sleep.'

CHAPTER THIRTY

WIN-WIN

Lorkan stands in the doorway of Serra's hut watching her hurriedly put a few things into her leather pack. 'You can't go out there alone, Serra. If the Lost Boys catch you, they will do worse than they did before, you know that. Wait. Wait till I'm back and the other tribes are here and maybe you can follow us, keep out of sight.'

'If you want to help, come with me. If not, stop speaking.'

'I can't... you know that. My time with the older warriors is coming. If I defy the elders I won't get it and I will be cast out. I have to leave for the other villages.'

'So stop speaking.' She opens up a box and begins to take out a series of weapons, clothes, a fire pouch.

'You can't do this, Serra.'

'What? So I go out and do what the warriors of this village are supposed to do?'

'They said you will get your revenge, they'll bring them back here, that's the agreement.'

'I made no agreement. I want to see them, look into their eyes, see the same fear they saw in mine.'

Lorkan sits on the bed in defeat. 'You can't do this alone.'

'That's why I'm going to find the one who helped me. He helped me then and he'll help me again. I know it.'

'Who is this man?'

'Maklan of the Deer Tribe.'

'Where is he?'

'I don't know. But the Hill will.'

'Serra, I'm frightened you'll get hurt, that something worse will happen to you. What about father? He told you to stay.'

'Don't worry about me, Lorkan. I'll be safe, I promise.' Serra ties the knot on her leather bag, slings it over her shoulders and ties it round her waist. She walks over to Lorkan, looks him in the eye for a moment then kisses him on the forehead. 'This is win-win. I'll be fine, I promise.'

'I pray to every god under the sun you are right.'

Serra walks to the doorway of the hut. Kera jumps off the bed and pads over to her, pressing her body against Serra's legs, looking out of the hut with her. They watch a group of villagers walking past. Serra waits for the path to clear then walks silently out, Kera close to her, and slides round the back of the hut, to the edge of the village and the hidden hole she and Lorkan used to climb through as children. In a few seconds, she is gone.

CHAPTER THIRTY ONE

HUNTED

Maklan stumbles on a small boulder. 'Slow down, Tenmar!'

Tenmar stops to see if Maklan is alright. 'We keep moving this slow we'll never get there. I'm not going to lead you into a swamp, brother. I know where I'm going.'

'We've been walking for hours and I still can't smell the river. We should be at the river by now.' Maklan rubs his foot, stands and continues to follow his brother.

'We're not going to the river. Taking the long way round.'

'Why we taking the long way round?'

'Safer. You said you wanted to do this, so we do it my way. I'm the one with the eyes, so you follow me, we find Sanfar then we go home.'

Maklan trips on a series of jagged rocks poking out of the well-worn path. He curses the ground, Tenmar and his blindness. 'Not this route, brother, the ground's too rough.'

'We can head back anytime you like.' Tenmar stops and shortens the length of rope linking him and his brother, then continues on at a slower pace, keeping his eyes straight ahead, vision wide, taking in everything he can. 'How do you know this Jacob Hill will be any help in finding Sanfar?'

Maklan takes out some liquorice root, bites off a chunk and hands it to Tenmar, he speaks through a mouthful of liquorice pulp. 'He'll know how to find him.'

'What about father?'

'What about him?' Maklan spits the liquorice pulp on the ground and wipes his mouth.

'While we're out here, maybe we could look for him too?'

'Not me.' Maklan watches a hare move noisily through the shrub ahead of them. 'You can find him when we have Sanfar. I don't want anything to do with him.' Maklan spits on the ground again.

'You need to make peace with our father. He's a mess but he's still our father. It wasn't always so bad.'

'I'm done with him. Ever since I felt the spade hit my face.'

' Tenmar speeds up the pace, Maklan follows. 'There's a wood ahead, we get to that, I'll build us some shelter and get us some food.'

'Let me hunt. I can do it blind. Be good practice.'

Tenmar walks on toward the distant tree line with Maklan close behind.

They reach the edge of a darkened wood and head in zigzagging through head-high boulders and thickets of gorse, hazel and heather.

Hidden eyes follow the two brothers as they enter the pine-wood, scanning them carefully, taking in every scrap of information about their movement, size, height and possible strength. This silent hunter can take down four men their size with ease. He's been tracking Tenmar and Maklan since sunrise, sent out from the Lost Boy Tribe to hunt down any potential threats. He takes his bow from his back, an arrow from the quiver and brings the two together, tightening bowstring back to firing position, lining up arrow tip with Maklan's head; he lets his aim dip an inch to Maklan's exposed neck, kneeling down deeper into firing position, pushing his knee into the soft ground to steady himself. He has a few seconds to fire before he loses the shot. He brings his weapon slowly round, following the footfall of his prey, index finger beginning to tremble at the tension held on the string of the bow. He gently lowers his weapon and exhales, lies down in the heather and disappears from sight. He knows who Maklan is and what he's done. He will wait till he can get closer, enjoy watching the last moments of his life flicker and die from his eyes for bringing dishonour to his men and taking his woman.

The brothers disappear into the shadows of the wood. The hunter waits a moment then rises slowly from the thicket. He creeps forward silent and low, following the far line of the wood, keeping out of the presence of any birds that could send warnings and give him away. The wood is thick and hard going.

Tenmar slows the pace. 'Keep your head low brother, don't want your eyes any worse.'

Maklan does as he's told, one hand ahead, feeling his way. He thinks of Serra. The image of her leaving him on the hillside flashes into his mind. He wonders what happened when she went back to her village, what the warriors of her tribe decided. They will no doubt come to the Lost Boy Tribe. And there will be blood.

CHAPTER THIRTY TWO

SEEKING JUSTICE

Serra walks silently on, comfortable in buckskin sandals thin enough to let her feet shape themselves to the land with ease. Kera stays close, alert, eyes on everything. Serra knows this land like a sister, it's part of her. She knows its seasons, animals; where, when and how they live, when's the right time to kill them; where to get berries, roots, leaves and medicine. Her mother took her out in this same landscape when she was a small child, day and night, sunshine, rain, snow, wind. She learned the language of the land before she learned the language of her tribe. The language of wind, river, earth, plant, sky, animal. She moved freely through the woods and across moor until her first moonbleed. On that bright, cold day, frost on the ground, snow in the air, she was taken in silence to a hut on the edge of the village by the elder women. They sat in a circle around her in the small dark space made only for women. Serra remembers the warm, welcome space, filled with wood-smoke and bright shards of light. She was given iron medicine from nettles and freshly cooked deer, caught by her father, iron to replace the lost blood. They told her of the future of her life as a woman, what she would have to do in the village. Her place in it. What strengths she had, what weaknesses. They told her of all the good she had already done for the tribe. The kindness she showed her tribe-brothers and sisters, her blood family, how she was already a skilled medicine woman even at the age of only twelve summers. She feels the memory of the darkness of the space, the eyes of women she could not fully see. She felt their attention, wisdom and instruction. She remembers the Seeing Stones cast down in front of her on the dark earth floor. Ancient stones holding gateway knowledge to the future. The same crone who said she couldn't join the search party earlier that day, looked long and hard at the rough-edged crystal rocks. 'You will be a great tracker, a hunter and a warrior and one day perhaps, a leader, but you will not be without pain and hardship and heartache. You must use this pain to grow or it will swallow you up and turn you into one of the outsiders... the dark ones.'

Serra listened without saying a word. She never believed the bit about becoming a leader. She knew she had something to give, something to contribute to help the village grow. She knew she had a rightful place. They told her of the connection of seasons, of marriage, birth, war, death and men. 'Any man who comes to you, must by right of village law show you respect, to honour you and your place in the tribe. If he moves too fast, he must be scolded. Give him clear warning. If he doesn't listen, kick him where his seed is carried. But you must not draw blood. No one must die for any crime committed to our tribe or for any wrongdoing. Be tough only to defend yourself and to teach lessons where they must be learnt. You are beautiful Serra and your beauty will deepen before it weakens. It will bring strong, fine-looking warriors to your hut, but it will also bring trouble. Bees sometimes eat too much honey, they get drunk on the nectar and lose their way home! Show them your mind, strength and heart. That will force respect beyond groping hands and fumbling fingers of boys not yet worthy to call themselves men.'

Serra walks on toward the setting sun. The high hills surrounding and marking the boundary of her village come steadily into view and, with the sight of them, her heart lifts. Kera looks up at her, questioning, waiting, eager to keep moving. Serra moves swiftly over rock, boulder, thicket and stream, Maklan in her mind, and seeking justice for her heart, in her heart. Kera follows close behind.

CHAPTER THIRTY THREE

THE ARROW AND THE NIGHT

Tenmar and Maklan reach a wide clearing in the wood. Along one side is a stream and close to that, the ruins of an old stone hut, its roof long gone.

'We may have found our shelter, brother.'

They walk to it.

'What? What is it?'

'An old ruin. No roof, but its walls are still intact and will keep the wind off. I can fix something for a roof for us, plenty of bracken and branches about.'

'Take me to it.'

Tenmar leads Maklan to its walls and unties the rope. Maklan runs his fingers slowly over the old stones, using its walls as a guide round its short perimeter.

Tenmar heads back to the edge of the wood and begins to gather dead wood and standing bracken from last season, brown and dry. He heaps his harvest near the walls of the ruin and heads back to find the skeleton branches and twigs that will build the roof.

Maklan sits down inside the shell of the building. He feels the soft welcome of rest in his legs and sits back against the cold stone. He looks up, sensing the shift in light as it seeps in through his scabbed eyes, rising from the dark of the ground to the light of the clear sky.

'What's the weather like?' he asks Tenmar.

'Clear, not a cloud. Blue sky. Any better?'

'What?'

'Your eyes?'

'Same. Some outlines, not much.'

'Think it'll come back?'

'No idea.' Maklan runs his hands through his hair.

'Who brought you back to the village?'

'No idea. Like to think it was Jacob, but I doubt it.'

Tenmar continues to find and stack the branches and bracken. 'We'll need leaves. Lots of leaves.'

Maklan stands up, looking around him, as if his eyes were working. He smells the air, listens for the sounds.

Tenmar stops what he's doing. 'What is it?'

'We should move. Find somewhere else to sleep.'

'Don't be stupid. Where we going to go this time of day? Be dark soon. I'm not letting all this work go to waste. This is a good spot.'

'We should get back into the wood, out of sight. We're too exposed.'

'Your dead eyes making you more scared than usual?' Tenmar smiles. 'Go find us some food.'

Maklan was up for hunting but the memory of the stag and the current bad feeling in his gut has changed his mind. Something lands at his feet. He jumps back. 'What is that?!'

'Easy, Storm Catcher. Rabbit snare. Get us some dinner - or at least breakfast. We have enough dried meat for tonight but we'll run out soon.'

Maklan picks up the trap and walks away from the ruined building. He uses his ears to find the tree line. The movement of leaves gets louder. He keeps one searching hand ahead of him. The sound of Tenmar building the shelter fades. He feels the presence of the trees. It gets cooler around him. His fingers reach the first tree trunk. He moves on, swinging his hands in a wide arc, walking slowly into the densely-packed trees. The sounds around him change immediately. The wind drops, cooler on his skin. He crouches down feeling the texture of the earth. He stands and continues to move forward, slowly, bringing his hand up every few feet to check for trees, boulders and bushes.

He reaches a much smaller clearing and works his way round it. He drops onto his hands and knees and searches for the small, familiar pellet droppings. It takes a good ten minutes but he finds what he's looking for. He continues to search the ground with blackened fingers. He comes to the small, cool opening of what he knows is a rabbit hole. The air is colder around it. He begins to lay his snare, quiet as he can. He knows this routine off by heart, done it a hundred times. Rabbit is not the best of food but it's easy to catch - once you've found the warren. He feels good. Proud. He can do this alone. They won't starve. Not tomorrow, or the next day.

He stands and walks back the way he came. A blast of wind hits him in the back. He stops and listens. The feeling of danger returns, louder and stronger than before. His skin starts to prickle. The wood surrounding him quickly becomes threatening. Without thinking, he walks straight ahead, fast. In less than ten seconds he walks straight into a tree. The impact knocks him to the ground. He sits there, long enough to get his breath, fear rising in his gut. He gets quickly back onto his feet, unsteady, dizzy. He walks forward again, slower now. His shoulder clips the side of a big gnarly tree. He moves more cautiously. The sticky heat of blood steadily covers his shoulder, followed by the dull thump of the fresh wound. He hears the break of a twig ahead and stops dead in his tracks. He brings his breathing down low and slow. He crouches down, listening in every direction.

He waits.

Nothing.

Then more footfall. He reaches down and slides out his blade from his leg binding.

A hand rests gently on his shoulder. He swings wildly round. The figure behind him easily steps clear of his blade.

'Easy, bro, easy.'

'TENMAR! What are you doing?!?'

'You'll have someone's eye out with that.'

'What you doing, creeping up on me like that?!'

'Came to see how you were doing. Heard a thump, thought you'd walked into a tree.'

Maklan shakes his head. 'Well I did. Ripped my shoulder open. Help me up.' Tenmar helps him to his feet, guides him safely out of the wood.

The bad feeling inside Maklan remains.

———

Maklan and Tenmar sit close to the fire they've built inside the walls of the ruined hut. Maklan feels around the torn cloth covering his shoulder. The makeshift roof is built and the weather has remained clear. Stars begin to appear one by one. Tenmar looks over to Maklan who stares blindly into the flames of the fire, enjoying its warmth but unable to see its fiery orange sparking into the blue-black night. He feels sorry for him. He tears the last piece of dried deer meat in two, hands one to Maklan, puts his in his mouth and begins to chew.

'Stars any good?' Maklan asks.

'Nothing special. It's getting cold. I'll build up the fire.' He stands and heads over to the pile he gathered earlier. Something stops him.

'What? What is it?' Maklan asks.

'Thought I heard something... over near the tree line.'

Maklan stands. 'I'm sure there's something out there. Feels like someone's been watching us all day.'

'I'll go look.' Tenmar loads a pile of wood onto the fire.

'I'll come with you.'

'It'll be quicker if I go. Probably just fox or badger smelling the meat.'

Tenmar heads out. The warmth of the fire soon leaves his back and the coldness of the night envelops him. He would prefer not to be doing this.

He reaches the tree line and stops, spooked by the darkness. He looks back to the now distant red glow of the fire licking up above the walls of the old house. He sees the silhouette of Maklan's dark outline looking in his direction, trying to see into the dark through the dark of his own blindness. Tenmar turns back to face the black interior of the wood. He steps into the inky darkness, feeling the wood surround him front, back and side. He stops to listen. Nothing. The wind is gentle in the leaves and trees, a constant soft whisper but no comfort. He takes a step forward. The hidden figure is revealed in the grunt of the running attack coming at him. Tenmar is paralysed. He must make a decision immediately. No longer concerned with the silence of the hunt, rapid crunching of footfall on dead leaves comes at him from behind. A few twigs snap and echo through the wood. Sounds come at him so fast he is unable to react quick enough, no time to turn around, no time to get his blade out. He steps to the side and ducks down into the darkness. The split-second waiting is over. The impact on his back is sudden, massive and crushing. He let's out an involuntary cry of pain. The air is pushed from his lungs by the massive weight bearing down on him. By the time his face hits the forest floor he is already beginning to drown in the mass of wet, rotten leaves. He feels the big human hand come down onto the back of his head ramming his face into the decomposing leaves, using their suffocating mulch as a weapon. Tenmar has fight in him. He will fight, but he knows in his bones that this is his time.

Maklan leans into the darkness as if he'd be able to make out more of the alien sounds he heard. Something has attacked Tenmar, he knows it. He heard his brother's cry of pain fly out of the darkness. The sickening sound that followed, the hard thud of body against body. He knows the line ahead to the trees is clear. He could run it, sprint for the wood. Stop at the tree line. Wait for whatever it is to come out to him. He'll have his blade ready. He hesitates. Readies himself. Gets his blade out. Another cry comes from the wood. It is Tenmar.

Tenmar's arms are pinned to the ground, his right hand held down fast. There is movement in his left arm. He begins to wriggle it free.

'No sense in moving now, is there?' The hunter snarls down at him.

Tenmar feels the point of something sharp in the back of his neck. Not a blade, a much sharper point. An arrowhead.

'You have the one you are with to thank for this.'

'What are you talking about?'

'Escaped from our village with one of our women. If you're with him, you pay… just as he will.'

Tenmar twists his body and pushes back up with all his strength. The weight on him doesn't shift more than a few inches. He gives it one last try, one last twist, adrenaline refuelling his rapidly fading strength. He manages to get onto his side. The crushing weight of his attacker coming down on his exposed ribs and stomach. He gasps in lungfuls of air, fighting against the loss of breath.

'Feisty one, aren't you?' The hunter brings his face close to Tenmar's. 'You stink of fear. Just like your brother, first night I saw him on the edge of our village and I took his pissy little blade from him. You have something in common.' The hunter smiles. 'You're both shit-for-nothing, useless fighters.'

Tenmar rests a second, tries to get back some strength. His legs are almost free. He pushes his knee down into the earth, pushes up with his body and frees his left leg. He brings it up hard into the lower spine of the hunter. The big, dirty, hairy attacker lets out a growl of pain and rage, then brings his focus back down onto his prey, pushing Tenmar's face back down hard into the leaves. He picks up the dropped arrow and looks at its glistening tip. He brings it back to Tenmar's neck.

'Where you want this? Your choice. It's going in somewhere. Neck's the second quickest. Or here? This is fast, not so much pain... so I'm told.' He jabs the arrowhead just below Tenmar's armpit and pushes it slowly into the thin flesh between his ribs. Tenmar winces but holds back any sound. He can just see the hunter's blackened teeth grinning through the darkness, his warm, putrid breath reeking out of him. 'What's it to be then... runt boy? Least I can do is give you a choice... eh?'

'Why don't you crawl back to your mother... see if she can forgive herself for producing such a pitiful bitch...?'

The hunter brings the arrow back up to his lip to shush Tenmar. 'Ah ah. Never insult the mother. Everyone knows that. Get yourself killed for less.' Tenmar tries again to move but the weight of the man on top of him is suffocating and so full of force he is left paralysed.

Tenmar feels death coming close to him. 'Do your worst, runt bitch. I'll haunt you and fill you with nightmares till your death breath, promise you that.'

'I reckon the neck.' The arrow is brought up beneath Tenmar's chin, to the point between his jaw and neck. The hunter places his hand over Tenmar's mouth. The arrow is pushed gently but firmly in as he holds his face close to Tenmar's, looking him straight in the eye. Tenmar feels the point pierce the skin, sliding in deep. 'Shhhh.' The hunter mock soothes Tenmar's death journey as if putting a child to sleep. The pain that follows the driving wooden arrow shaft burns and sears far into his head. He lets go into it. As he begins to surrender into a final blackness he hears the crashing whack of a body against trees, bushes and boulder, the rush and rustle of leaves followed by the war cry of his brother. The grip on the arrow shaft loosens. Tenmar's eyes snap open. He sees the familiar shadow outline of Maklan pulling the hunter off him, onto the forest floor. The fighting, flailing shadows merge in the darkness, arms and legs fly, each trying to get the upper hand on the other. Maklan's skinny body moves fast over the startled hunter like a black spider, comfortable in the blackness of its night-time world, wrapping itself round prey way too big, impossible to kill. Tenmar hears the mixed grunts and quick, sharp breaths of the two warriors, lurching between tree and bush, whacking into wood and gorse, cracking smaller branches, snapping twigs, crashing through bracken. Maklan is thrown to the thorny ground. Tenmar knows what he must do if he's to make his last moments on earth count, make his death mean something. He won't survive this wound, not so far from home, he knows that for sure; there is no medicine out here that will pull him back from the death shadow that now covers him in a suffocating, borderless mass. He reaches his hand up to his neck, to the arrowhead. He brings his fingers round the shaft and grips it tight. He whispers his final resolution.

'For the tribe. For you, brother.'

He draws the arrow out, inch by body-shattering inch with a low howl like the whine of a beaten, dying wolf.

The fighting shadows stop and look back for a confused, exhausted split second into the darkness where Tenmar lies, gasping, sobbing. He forces his final words from his clenched lips. 'Bring the bitch to me, bro.'

Maklan, not thinking, not questioning, blind in rage and sight, roars out his final burst of strength, pushing up against the hunter's weight, jamming his body into him, forcing him toward the sound memory of his brother's voice. The hunter falls to the ground. Maklan jumps on him and does what he can to hold him down. The struggle continues. The hunter roars, bringing his mouth to Maklan's leg, sinking teeth into calf flesh, skin ripping, splitting, blood instantly drawn. Maklan screams. In this moment, the moment where dirty black teeth bite deeper into Maklan's leg, in the spinning confusion of shouting and violence, writhing, rageful limbs, Tenmar rises up with the last energy of his life, bringing the arrow up hard and fast into the hunter's neck, driving it through flesh and muscle until it emerges the other side. The hunter opens his mouth, releases Maklan's leg, tips his head back and makes to scream.

Silence.

His vocal chords now belong to the arrow and the night.

He falls onto his back, eyes wide, staring up at the stars blinking down at him between the dark canopy of leaves. Tenmar slumps back, sharing the final deathwatch vision of bright white stars.

The two warriors draw their final air of this world, moments apart.

The forest is silent save Maklan's searching, panicking breath. The silence is broken by his wailing grief as he finally finds and takes hold of the lifeless body of his brother.

Chapter Thirty Four

DEATH MASK

Sanfar stares down into the water, transfixed by his reflection, frightened at how much his face has changed, thinner, sicker, paler. His body feels weak, his mind scattered. The silverine sickness in him again. However much he takes there is always a need for more, somewhere deep in his bones. He puts his fingers into the cold water and swipes his reflection away, hoping it will rub him out for real. The water settles down. His rippling, skeletal face comes into view.

'Look at this 'ere then. Doesn't the little one look all serious?'

Sanfar's thoughts are broken by the familiar rasping of Bones' irritating voice. He turns to look at him.

'What you want, Bones?' It's not a question he really wants answering.

Bones walks up to the water's edge and takes out a pipe. A string of smoke trickles out from the still-burning silverine inside the white clay bowl. He brings it to his lips and sucks, keeping his eyes on Sanfar, grinning.

Sanfar fidgets, aching muscles screaming for the drug. He wants to smash Bones' face in. The chance of some silverine makes him clench his fists but he resists. He gets up from the water's edge and stands, facing Bones. Bones takes the pipe from his lips, eyelids drooping a little, head tilting back up to the sky, as if he just went to another place. A grin of pleasure spreads across his pockmarked face. He opens his eyes and brings his attention back to Sanfar 'Want some?' He holds the pipe out to him.

'Stop playing games. You know I do.' Sanfar gets up and steps forward.

Bones withdraws the pipe. 'Ah, ah. Not so fast. Zed wants you to do another thing for him.'

'What thing?'

'Best you take your blade with you again.'

'I'm not getting any more coin back. I'm done with that.'

'Then you're done with this.' Bones shows him the pipe, as if he needed reminding.

'You can keep your stinking pipe. Not doing it.'

'Zed won't be happy to hear that.'

Something snaps inside Sanfar. Like the last twig on the branch of a dead willow. 'Tell Zed I'm finished here.' He pauses. 'In fact, tell Zed he's as dead to me as you are.'

Bones smiles. 'Be happy to tell him that. But you know he won't be happy to hear it. I look forward to seeing you strung up, begging for silverine and a rusty blade to sink into any scum who hasn't given us what's owed.' Bones takes a long draw on the pipe till it crackles and burns, sucking in deep the dregs of the drug. He looks at the pipe, then drops it into the mud and stamps it down hard, till it disappears. He turns and walks away slowly, meandering from left to right, whistling a tune Sanfar doesn't recognise. When he finally vanishes into the tree line, Sanfar bends down and tries to dig the pipe out of the mud. He finds it, puts it quickly to his lips and sucks. Nothing but dead, black ash.

'I SEE YOU!' Bones shouts. 'DON'T THINK I DON'T SEE YOU!!' Bones' laugh echoes through the darkness of the wood.

Sanfar turns and drops the dead pipe into the water. He kneels down and brings his gaze back to the ripples as they reach out in wider and wider rings into the lake. He watches them settle, waits for his pale, death-mask face to appear. The mirror-stillness of the water returned, he sees and hates himself a little more.

CHAPTER THIRTY FIVE

DIG DIG DIG

Why do I have to be blind? What in Thunor's name am I supposed to do? I'm done, finished, dead for sure.

Maybe he's not dead.

'Don't be stupid. You felt his heart, nothing; listened for breath, nothing.' *Talking to yourself won't help. It's been three hours now, no movement. He's gone. He's gone and it's your fault.*

He can't be.

He's gone. You need to bury him. And you need to get rid of the other body, hide it.

What am I supposed to do? Not going back. Can't go on. Can't leave him here. How do I get out of this wood blind? I'm finished. Never going to find Sanfar. I'll starve out here. Be eaten by wolves.

Get up.

Bury your brother.

He must be burned to ash by the elders. That's the way.

You can't get back on your own, can't drag him back. You leave him here they'll be eating him in a matter of hours.

I want to take him home, back to the village.

You can barely walk without smashing into a tree.

'No. Not putting him in the ground. Not covering him with earth.'

He's dead. Put him in the ground and say your goodbyes. Make a ritual for him. Send him off to the death place in a good way. Do that, then get rid of the other one and find Jacob. He's your only hope.

Flies around him already and he's still warm.

Can't do this.

You need something to dig with. Wood, stone. Here. Pointed rock.

Dig. Slow. Keep your strength. Dig a hole for your brother.

He gave his life for you now put some life into saying goodbye to his.

Dig.

Dig.

Dig.

———

Must get some food. Rabbit from last night. Water. Last food we ate together. Last hunting we'll do.

'Need to keep going. Nearly done. Hole is big enough.'

Rest a bit... before you do it.

I can't do this. Can't put him in the ground. What if he's still alive? What if he wakes up with all that earth over him?

He won't.

What if he does?

He won't.

If you'd taken him back to the village they'd have burnt him. This is better.

'It would be better if he was still alive.'

You can do this. One step at a time.

Raining. The earth'll get sticky.

Get him in the hole. His legs first.

Thunor, I can't do this.

Drag him in... slow.

He's heavier than I remember.

Dead weight.

Think I'm going to throw up.

'You can do this. You have to do this.'

So heavy.

Pull.

Harder.

That's it.

Now into the hole.

'Fffawrrrr'

He's breathing! He's alive! 'Tenmar! Tenmar!'

He's dead. Just the last of his air leaving his body because you're moving him. Saw that in the village with that old man when they put him on the pyre.

'This is too much. Can't do this.'

Keep going. He's nearly there. Nearly in the ground.

Legs.

Body.

Arms.

Head.

Too short. The grave is too short. Bend his legs a little, get his feet in.

That's it.

Now the earth.

Keep going.

Cover him.

Keep going.

Now the rocks.

Fingers hurting.

Keep going.

Nearly finished.
Last rock.
Now say what you have to say. Say your goodbye.
What am I supposed to say to you brother?

'I'm sorry? It should be me? Maybe it should. You saved me. The last thing you did was for me. You did some bad things to me when we were growing up, bullied me, but you were always there when I needed you, brother. You wanted to find our father, I know that. I came for Sanfar. You came for me, to protect me, and you died for me.'

Chapter Thirty Six

HELP

Maklan sits by Tenmar's grave, growing hungrier by the hour, unable to find the will to get up and move, to head home or ahead or get food. No idea which way to go. He sits and waits for a time he knows will never arrive. He holds the arrow pulled from the Lost Boy's body, he looks down at it, at the red blood from his brother-killer and his brother, melded, blended, dried, gone black. He snaps the arrowhead off and puts it in his pouch. The dead Lost Boy lies in a shallow grave in the woods; deep enough to hide him from his brothers, shallow enough for the animals to dig into and eat at their leisure.

Memories of voices and conversations in his head merge with the known sounds of the wood. The wind in the trees, leaves and grass; easy birdsong high up and low down on the ground; the distant rumble of the river.

He senses the change before his mind has time to kick in and ask the question. He feels it in his body. He knows something is in the wood. Wonders if it is the ghost of the boy he killed, or another Lost Boy tribesman. He panics, unable to move. The soft crunching footfall on last season's dead, dry leaves builds in volume as the figure approaches him.

'What do you want?' Maklan asks, shaking from cold, hunger and fear. 'Leave me in peace to grieve.'

The footfall stops close to him. Silence follows. A hand rests on his shoulder. Maklan flinches.

'Who is buried here?'

Maklan recognises the voice instantly and his spirits rise. 'Jacob?' But his heart quickly sinks again. He replies in a half mumble. 'My brother. Tenmar.'

Jacob sits down next to him. 'What happened here?'

Maklan tells him, detail by detail. Tears in eyes and throat. Jacob listens without interruption. Maklan talks for over an hour until his throat is dry, belly raw and growling with hunger.

'You're hungry. Come. I'll take you back to my hut. There's hot food in the pot. The hut is a few hours from here. Can you walk?'

Maklan nods. 'How did you find me?'

'You were easy to find. It was time.'

'Why did you help me back to my village?'

'You'd be dead if I hadn't.'

Maklan is silent for a moment. 'Will I be blind forever?'

'What can you see?'

'Shapes. Not much. Can find my way around places I know but out here... I'm lost. Can you give me more medicine?'

'I don't know if it will help. You need to get strength back in your eyes. This is a physical wound. There is no promise of your sight coming back.'

'I'll do anything, whatever I have to... I have to find Sanfar, have to see him again.'

Maklan looks down at the blackened blur of Tenmar's grave and feels tears well up. He lifts his head up to the light. Outlines and shapes of what he believes are trees are blurred further by the stinging tears in his eyes. He closes them and sinks his head to his knees.

Jacob speaks softly. 'Your grieving will be long. Death is never easy. You will come through.'

'He gave his life for me. I should be in the ground, not him.'

'It was his time... not yours. You need rest so your eyes can heal.'

Maklan feels the rough fur of Jacob's dog come up to him and bury his nose in his chest. He ruffles his coarse hair and puts both his arms round him.

They rise together. Jacob and the dog walk a few yards ahead. Maklan follows the reassuring outline of their bodies.

The walking pace Jacob sets is slow. He keeps to a simple even path. They walk in silence for the first hour. Maklan enjoying the feeling of safety ahead, happy to be moving, trying to keep Tenmar out of his mind and his focus ahead, on Sanfar.

Jacob finally speaks. 'Tell me about this tribe-brother of yours, Sanfar.'

'He left our village last full moon.' Maklan pauses, swallowing hard. 'We fought... argued. He was in a bad place. He will be in an even worse one now. I know it. I have to find him.'

'He came to my hut.'

'What?'

'His visit was short. He said he was looking for Heartfall. I sent him in that direction.'

'Why didn't you tell me? That's why I came here...'

'I told you what you needed to hear.'

'Being attacked and blinded is the right place to be then?'

Jacob is silent. Maklan stares at his back long and hard. 'If I can stay with you, till I get enough sight back.'

'You can stay, but you need to know your sight may never return.'

'Can you show me how to fight... blind? Wherever Sanfar has gone... I'll need to know how to protect myself.'

'If you can't see clearly you won't get further than a few miles before someone or something tries to eat you or rob you.'

'I have nothing to steal.'

'Perhaps you should return home. I can take you.'

'My father is as good as dead to me. My brother dead and buried. I need to find Sanfar. You are all I have to make that possible.'

Jacob falls silent, continuing to lead the way.

CHAPTER THIRTY SEVEN

DEEP WATER

Four sunrises later

'Fu-fu-ffreeezing. Ca-can't do it again! Not going down there again.'

'You said you were prepared to do anything, Maklan.'

'This is stupid. How is this going to help me?! I don't even know what I'm looking for down there. I thought you were training me to fight blind.'

'You'll know it when you find it. If you can't do this, you won't be able to defend yourself.'

'I'll drown if I go any deeper.'

'There is always more breath left in there somewhere. You just have to want to find it.' Jacob smiles at him. 'You'll know what it is when you find it.'

'Hey! Don't poke me with that stupid stick… stop pushing me.' *Thunor no. Not again. This water is so cold! Never gets easier. Third time. Bet he never did this. The rocks he put in my pockets drag me down faster every time.*

Get them out then.

Deeper, getting darker again.

Get the rocks...

Too late. Too deep. All black again.

Lungs almost empty...

Find it and get back to the hut, fire, food.

Lungs hurting. Hands and feet numb... blood feels like... mud...

Behind the biggest boulder, that's what he said.

This one's bigger than the others. Swim round it, round the back.

Something back here. A hole. A cave.

I'm not going in there.

He said a cave. This is a cave. Swim in. Find it.

Swim into it, find whatever it is and finish his stupid game.

No air. Lungs killing me. Feels like I'm dying down here.

There's always more. That's what he said.

What if there's something in there? Something alive?!

There's nothing down there except fish bones.

So black.

Everyone's blind down here.

But I've found a new sense, in the black, like in the wood, before Jacob came. Use it. Find this thing. Get back before... my lungs explode.

Swim forward.

You can do this.

Weeds...

... everywhere.

No monster down here.

No breath. Skin on fire.

Rock wall. Back of cave. Slimy. Hard.

Something here.

Hilt. Hilt of a sword...

Stuck.

Pull harder.

Not coming.
Pull. Gently.
It's free.
Get back.
Get these rocks out.
Swim. Swim hard.
No breath.
Sword so heavy.
Swim.
No air. Killing me.
No death down here.
Light.
I can see light through water
A figure on the bank
It's him.
Jacob.

Chapter Thirty Eight

ANCIENT BLADE

The rusted tip of the sword breaks the surface of the water, followed by the rest of its ancient, heavy metal; then Maklan's arms, body and legs as he scrabbles and gasps and collapses onto the tiny shingle beach. He hears the deafening roar of the waterfall behind him. The constant pounding of water on stone that took centuries to form the deep black hole he's just been to the bottom of, and come back from, alive, just. Jacob Hill's warm hand is clasped round his. He pulls him up onto the bank. Maklan struggles to stand and collapses in a heap, the battered, rusted weapon clenched tight in his hand. He looks up at the sky, seeing the silhouette of the rocks all around them. He draws in the clean fresh air like a newborn baby. Jacob sits close by, silent, waiting.

When the time is right, he helps Maklan up and they walk silently back through the wood to the hut, hearth, fire and food.

———

Maklan sits on the edge of his bed, looking at the rusted blade, frowning, trying to see it through half blindness. He runs his fingers down its rough edge. It snags and cuts his finger.

'Ow!' He shakes his head. 'This is useless. This is what I nearly died for?'

'Don't be fooled by the rust and jagged edge.'

'Felt better underwater. Too heavy. How am I meant to fight with this?' He stands up and holds the sword up above his head trying to make out its shape. The tip of the blade goes through the wattle-and-daub roof of the hut. A shaft of light rushes down the rust-red metal. He feels the heat of the sun warm his skin. He looks apologetically back at Jacob. 'Sorry. I'll fix that.'

Jacob says nothing.

Maklan draws the blade back from the bright sky outside and lays it down on his bed. 'It nearly killed me.'

'You wouldn't be the first.' Jacob stirs the pot of stew, picks up a handful of deer meat and drops it into the boiling liquid. The hut is quickly filled with the sweet aroma of cooking meat and vegetables.

'Was it used in a fight, in battle?'

'Many.'

Maklan picks the sword up again looking at it in a different light, trying to make out more of its details. 'Has it seen blood? How long has it been down there?' Jacob continues to stir the pot and speaks, not looking at Maklan.

'I cast it down there a long time ago.'

'What for? Did you kill someone? Is that why you're out here alone?'

Jacob looks at Maklan, no expression. 'My father did the killing. In battle...'

Maklan sits down on the bed and lays the blade down as if it were an animal he respects but can no longer trust.

Jacob continues. 'I had another one like you... came here ten summers ago. Sent him down to get it. He tried three times.

Failed three times. It's good to see it again. I didn't think it would be.'

'Why did you want it back after all this time?'

'I thought the memories would sink with it.'

Maklan shivers at the memory of being in the liquid darkness and the death he'd felt all around him.

Jacob takes out two wooden bowls and serves up the hot stew. He fills both bowls to the brim and hands one to Maklan and sits down in his chair.

Maklan stares at the blurred outline of his mentor, waiting for him to say something. The smell of the stew rises up into his nose. Jacob looks into his bowl, steam rising up, covering his face. He murmurs a prayer to the food. Maklan dips his head and mutters the same words.

They sit and eat in silence.

———

Maklan breaks the silence. 'Did you know your father?'

Jacob shakes his head and looks into the fire. 'I lived with my mother, in the forests of the north moor for most of my younger years. We saught refuge there after my father was killed. A wild, desolate place with few people. Cold and harsh even in the summer months.'

'Who killed your father?'

'A warlord after he had killed the warlord's son in battle. That is what I was told. His sword made its way back to my mother after passing through many hands. She buried it in the woods soon after we came. She wanted nothing more to do with war and the death it brings.' Jacob looks down at the earth floor of the hut as if watching a memory unfold. 'She went insane with grief. When I was old enough I finally left her and the place we had lived. She had always warned me of the danger of men beyond the

woods, so I dug up the old blade and made it ready.' Jacob looks at
the ancient blade lying next to Maklan. 'They say she died of grief.
I realised after three years on path, moor and ocean why she kept
me in the forest, hidden. But I had to find that out for myself. The
world beyond this place is full of violence and senseless death.'
Jacob falls silent for a moment, eating, thinking. He finishes his
meal, puts the bowl down and wipes his mouth. 'So I came here,
found the waterfall and decided this land was good enough to
hunt and forage. The winters are not as harsh as in the north.
This is a wild place but safe from the anger and violence of men...
for now. You need only your wits to protect you from wolf and
bear. I no longer needed the swords protection, only the hunting
weapon of snare and bow. So I cast the ancient blade into the falls.'

'Why did you send me down there to get it back?'

'You'll need more than your dagger to get Sanfar home.'

'I don't understand.'

'If he's gone to Heartfall, it'll only be a matter of time before
his choices run out and he has to seek out the warlords for work.
And if he likes the mead he will soon be seeking out silverine.'

'Silverine?'

'The herb that keeps the warlords in place, keeps their work-
ers working, killing, robbing and thieving. It has torn Heartfall
apart. No one goes there unless they want lawlessness and death.
It's a city of the dead now. The walking dead. You'll need to get
him out of there if you don't want to bury another brother in the
ground.'

'How am I meant to do that blind?'

'First you get the blade back to what it was. Then I show you
how to use it. How you get to Heartfall is up to you. I'll keep giving you herbs that will help your eyes, but you'll need someone
with sight to take you. I can teach you to fight but I'm not taking
you.'

'I can't go alone. You said so yourself.'

'I can help you with the blade and the fighting.'

Maklan lets out a sigh of defeat and slumps back against the hut wall. 'You'll need to do something else as well... before you return to your village.'

Maklan looks up. 'What?'

'Find your father. Bring him back to your village.'

'I have no intention of doing that.'

'You will.'

'What?'

'Want to find him.'

'How can you be so sure?'

'Comes with age.'

Maklan picks up the sword and feels its weight.

'We start in the morning. If you refuse, then you must leave.'

Maklan looks at Jacob surprised. 'I have no choice?'

'You have a choice. You stay and learn to fight or you leave with nothing to protect you except your blade and instinct.'

CHAPTER THIRTY NINE

CALM BEFORE
THE STORM

'Come Kera. Time to run.' *I need to keep low. Avoid being seen by any of the other villagers on foot heading to the Lost Boy village. They'll be on their way by now. Lorkan and others from my tribe will be with them. And the village elders will be working out what to do with me when I get back. I need to keep moving. I must get to Maklan. I'll be at Jacob's hut soon, it's over the next ridge. What if I can't find him? You will; Jacob will help you.*

The wind on my face, my arms, neck, feels good. The rain cooling my skin. The sun breaking through the clouds up ahead. A rainbow over the tree line. The calm before the storm. It feels so good to be moving through the land. I need to eat. Jacob will have food.

Keep going.

'It's good to have you here, Kera.' *There's the ridge, a few yards more.*

There's another sound. Inside the wind. What is it? Grinding, like metal on stone. Someone is sharpening tools down there in the clearing beyond the ridge. That's Jacob's place. He's there... and he sounds busy.

Chapter Forty

BONE AND STONE

Maklan tries to make out the outline of Jacob working at the stone wheel. Born from the brutal meeting of blade on stone, he can just make out the sparks as they fly up into the air. Jacob's foot pumps rhythmically, driving the circle of stone at a steady speed, cutting into the burrs and rust on the ancient sword, revealing a cleaner new blade beneath.

'I work the first edge, you work the second.' He tells Maklan, concentration not moving from the work in hand.

'I'll cut my hand off with these eyes.'

'No you won't.'

Maklan crouches down and tunes his ears to the grinding sound. Metal on stone crafting the tools of war forces a memory he would rather bury forever. Days and nights by the fire of his father's forge, forced into learning through his once-good eyes. Long days and nights, blasted by the heat of the furnace, drying out his throat and lungs so much he could hardly speak. No food. His father would fall asleep, drunk on mead and heat. Maklan knew not to risk sneaking out to play with Tenmar. The beating given for the time he did made certain of that. The memory of his father's voice fills his mind, mixing with the sharpening blade under Jacob's steady hand. After all this time, the memory of his father's voice still fills Maklan with fear and dread. 'You'll stay there and learn. You don't have the skills you need to hunt so you'll stay there and watch and learn my trade and maybe one day you'll be good enough to make arrowheads.'

'When can I do what you do...?'

'You stay away from this fire until I say, you hear? Come near it and I'll beat you with this.' He seizes the red-hot poker. Memories are sharper; his mind always hunting, hungry for images from his past to make up for the loss of sight of the world in front of him now. He sees his father's hammer flattening metal on stone, held up at shoulder height, glinting red embers sparking on dull metal as the hammerhead beat the blades of war into shape. He sees the inside of the forge clear in his mind. The dark corners. The floor thick with dust and dirt, tools lying up against the side of the forge wall. Everything cast into deeper darkness by the harsh red light from the furnace. The sound of the bellows being pumped from outside by an exhausted Tenmar, half asleep, foot pushing up and down without thinking. Maklan and Tenmar trapped and separated by the forge wall and the shared fear of their father. For all his hatred of him, Maklan knew his father was a good blacksmith. The best in Devonia. Men would come from way up north to seek his weapons and have broken blades and axe heads made new. Men with great beards and huge wolfhounds at their side, a hunger for meat and mead and an eye for the women of the village. These were the only men Maklan was more terrified of than his father.

'Keep your eyes on the ground when they come. They catch you looking at them they'll take 'em clean out and there'll be nothing I can do to stop them, hear me boy? Keep your eyes on me and my work, nothing else.'

Maklan spent more time staring into the shadows of that forge than he did looking and learning how to mould metal into weapon. His mind always on the moors, learning to hunt with Sanfar and Tenmar. He searches for some kind of feeling toward his father, feelings other than hate. He finds none. He looks through his memory of the blackened forge, the hatred he grew to feel for every inch of its cramped, airless space; the hatred of its dark corners, the weapons, the tools, the heavy black apron his father had worn since before Maklan was born, tattered at the edges, stinking of fire and sweat. The suffocating heat, the lack of air. The hammering of iron on iron. The dull clank, clank, clank echoing in the deep dark rooms that hold these nasty, black memories. The sound of his old life, his village and his father are broken by the grinding of the blade against the stone in front him now, of Jacob whistling, of the birdsong surrounding him in the nearby trees and bushes. He is glad the memory is hammered back down, glad of the pleasure in the sound of an old, rusted, worn sword being made new. He even has a desire to work the iron himself.

The sound of blade against stone gets clearer. Clusters of sparks fly up in a fountain of white stars, thick and bright at the base, yellow and widening as they rise, arcing in a stream and landing at Maklan's feet. He reaches down to touch them but never gets to them before they fade into the earth.

Jacob finally stops and holds the half-sharpened blade up, looking at its edge for burrs of rusted steel and ridges from the hundreds of impacts on bone and stone. 'Your turn.'

Maklan rises to his feet and walks over, cautiously.

Jacob holds out the blade, hilt first. Maklan notices the reverence Jacob treats it with, sees the blur of the blade held steady in the old man's hand. With great respect, Maklan takes it. Jacob takes Maklan through the first simple stages of sharpening.

'First you say a prayer of thanks to the minerals that made the stone and the blade and then to the ritual of the meeting they will make, the coming together to reform it into the sacred object of war. Never rush this. The ancestors and spirits watch our work and they decide whether this is a righteous blade, to be used to preserve peace, protect lands and peoples from raiders. You do it right, your edge will be sharp.'

Maklan runs his thumb along the sharpened edge of the sword, feeling the razor line of iron trying to cut into his skin. He feels its power, like nothing he ever touched in his father's forge. He stops his thumb just before the skin slits open.

'Do it right, and this blade will cut through bone as if it were a sheath of grass. Do it wrong and it will break on the stone.'

Maklan is hesitant at first. Jacob steps back and watches from a distance.

Maklan brings the blade up and looks at it.

'What am I supposed to say to it?'

'Not it. Them. You say your prayer to the spirits and the ancestors.'

Maklan looks at the blade. 'Er... ancient blade of war... that's no good. What am I supposed to say? Help me. Help me bring this blade back, back to its old self. Take the rust of water from its edge, bring it back so I can get Sanfar back. Spirits and ancestors help me get this blade to shine.' Maklan brings the blade up above his head and holds it to the sky, turning it over, trying to make out the difference between Jacob's work and the water's rust. He runs his finger along it without thinking and cuts himself. He hopes Jacob hasn't seen. He has. He sucks his finger till it stops bleeding then lowers sword to stone. He brings his foot down on the wooden pedal, slowly working his foot up and down. The wheel turns. He picks up speed, holds firm. The sound of burrs being flattened and blade sharpened rings in his ears and makes him smile. All trace memories of his father and the forge and Tenmar vanish.

The blade slips. The surprise and weight of it pulls him forward. He stops himself from stumbling and falling over.

'Holding the blade steady's wiping me out.'

Jacob stays silent, watching.

He picks up the sword again, squinting hard to see the blurred outline of the stone in front of him. He rests the blade back down on its surface and brings his foot to the wooden paddle. He begins to pump his foot down, slowly at first, holding the blade steady.

'Come on, Maklan. You can do this,' he murmurs to himself.

He brings down a little too much pressure, tries to hold it back from coming off the stone again, slips and falls forward. He tries to right himself, pulling away from the still spinning stone but his cheek catches it, grazing the skin deep. It tears open. Blood comes quick. He falls to the ground howling. Jacob stands, watching for a moment.

Maklan brings his hand to his cheek and feels the blood seep into his palm.

Jacob steps forward. 'Put pressure on it, hold it. I'll get you something to put on it.'

'You can finish it yourself. That things has a life of its own.'

'You give up easy for a warrior.'

Maklan listens to the soft padding of Jacob's sandals on the wet ground as he walks away. He lies on his back, looking up at the sky. The water in the earth seeps into his shirt, cool against his skin. He pushes down harder on his cheek. He can feel the blood flow slowing and clotting. He looks up and squints harder to make out the shapes in the fast moving clouds above him. He sees something different in the sky. The clouds are clearer. He sits bolt upright and squints harder. 'I can see them! More of them. My eyes... I can see more of the outlines!'

'You have clearly lost your mind.'

Maklan's heart jumps with fright at the unexpected, female voice. Fear is replaced by excitement. He knows the voice. He could never forget it. 'Serra! Is that you?'

'Who'd you think it is? Have you forgotten what I look like already? Have you gone blind as well as losing your mind?' There is teasing in her voice.

Maklan stands up and looks around until his eyes fall on the familiar outline of Serra, the shape of her body, unable to see the details and features of the face he remembers. He steps forward, arms outstretched, searching.

Serra steps back. 'Stop messing around, I'm too tired for this.' Kera barks at him. Maklan keeps coming. Her irritation is quickly followed by alarm. As Maklan gets closer she makes out the scabs around his eyes and a fresh wound on his cheek. 'What's happened to your eyes?! Who did this to you?'

Maklan stops close to her and puts his hands on her shoulders. 'The stag took my eyes... I blame Jacob and his stupid stone for my face.' Kera sniffs at Maklan's feet. He bends down to stroke her.

'The Hill did this to your face? Are you blind?'

Maklan looks up at her. 'I was... I mean yes, it's coming back... my sight is coming ba...' Maklan stops mid flow, he listens to the return of Jacob, the familiar padding of his old sandals on the damp earth. Serra turns and looks at him. She takes out her blade. Kera barks at his approach. Serra steps forward, preparing to fight.

'Wait, Serra! Stop! I didn't mean he actually did this...'

Maklan sees the muted outline of Serra as she moves forward. 'Wait, Serra! STOP!!'

It doesn't take much for Maklan to work out that Serra is disarmed before she can get to within three feet of Jacob. In an instant he has taken her feet from beneath her and she is sitting, defeated, on the mud. Kera moves in to attack but is grabbed by the scruff of her neck, her legs paddling the air, growling, teeth snapping.

Jacob looks down at Serra. 'I wondered when you'd appear.'

'You knew she was coming?' Maklan asks, confused.

'You've been watching us for the last two hours. If I put your hound down will she stop?'

'Kera. Quiet.'

After a few seconds, the dog gives up, stops paddling and whines. Jacob puts her down. She runs over to Serra, sniffing, inspecting, licking.

'Why did you do this to him?' Serra looks up at Jacob, rage in her eyes.

'Whatever has happened to him has happened by his own hand and is exactly what he needs.' Jacob walks over to Maklan and looks at his wound. He brings an old cloth filled with a poultice to his face, gently pushing it into the cut. Maklan winces but lets him continue. 'Hold it firm,' he tells Maklan. Maklan brings up his hand and takes charge of the dressing. Jacob tears off a thin strip of cloth and with great care places it over the dressing and brings it round the back of Maklan's head. 'Turn around.' Maklan obeys, Jacob ties the knot.

'What are you doing here?' Jacob asks Serra.

'I came to find Maklan.'

Maklan touches the wound dressing, feeling the security of it. 'You came for me?' Questions fire through his mind like too many arrows. He can't get his tongue round any of them.

Serra stands and brushes herself down. 'I need your help... but it looks like you need it more than me.'

'Help for what?'

'The Lost Boys.'

CHAPTER FORTY ONE

WARMTH

Wish she'd come sit next to me. Warm me up. If I had the guts I'd go over there, sit next to her, put my arm across her shoulder.

Maybe just sit next to her.

I can feel her looking at me but can't see her. Need more wood on the fire.

This one. Big enough. Burn for a good time.

'Hey, watch where you're dropping that, Maklan of the Deer Tribe! Those sparks burn!'

That was a stupid thing to do. 'Would if I could, believe me… watch what I was doing.'

'Sorry, that was a stupid thing to say.'

'Don't worry.'

'Will you be able to remember where he's buried? I mean when you get your sight back?'

'Think so.' *If she came a bit closer maybe I could see more of her.*

'When are you going back to your village?'

'I'm not. Not yet.' *Maybe never.*

'But you have to tell the village. They have to perform the rituals or his spirit will stay in this realm, he'll get lost, he'll end up in the dark places.'

'You don't believe that, do you?'

'Of course I do. You don't?'

'Some of it. I did a ritual at his graveside. I think that's enough.'

'Think?'

'Felt like enough.' *You're sounding angry.* 'I'm sorry.'

'I understand.'

'Been angry for so long.'

'Can you fight?'

'If I can get close enough…'

'Then you can help me.'

'I'll slow you down. You're better off on your own.'

'I came here to get you… to ask you for help. I'm not leaving without you, even if you are as blind as a bat.'

You came here to get me.

Doesn't matter if you slow her down, you can be with her.

Maybe protect her if she gets attacked. 'I have to get Sanfar.'

'Where is he?'

'Heartfall.'

'How are you going to get there on your own?'

'Jacob's getting me ready. I'll ask him to take me some of the way.'

He's not taking you anywhere. You need her help. You help her, she'll help you and you get to be with her, as long as you like.

'If you come with me… to the Lost Boy Tribe and help me, I'll take you to Heartfall and help you find Sanfar. Neither of us can do what has to be done alone. If I don't get to them by sunrise tomorrow they will be taken by the other village warriors. I must get to them first.'

'Best we get some sleep then. Wake me before dawn, we'll have breakfast and leave at first light. *She's getting up. Walking over. Sitting next to me, lying down, her and Kera.*

I can feel her back against my legs.
Warming me up.
Warmth.
Time to sleep.

Chapter Forty Two

SEARCH PARTY

The tight formation of tracker warriors moves swiftly and silently through the blacked-out forest, the night and clouds making them almost invisible. They do not speak, only looking ahead, jogging at a steady pace, avoiding collision with the things of the forest, the trees, rocks, boulders, bushes. They've kept this pace for the last seven hours.

They came together in the furthest village south, the village closest to the sea. The surrounding villages had known for a good time of the boy tribe they are heading to now. They had put up with its night-raiding parties for the first two moons. There were many tribal meetings. Some of the villages sent scouts to track their movements. All returned with little to report other than the state of the village, the dirt, the chaos; too many fires burning and too much stripping of the ancient nearby trees for firewood. Everyone knew that without elders and older tribesmen, this is what happens, things get out of control fast. Eventually they sent a peace party to the Lost Boy village, a group of elders and warriors. They came to within a league of the village and were ambushed from the trees by a horde of fully-armed Lost Boys. Something had to be done. The villagers hoped they would tire of their makeshift village and eventually return home.

They did not tire and they did not return.

Lorkan and a group of men from his village joined up the tribes; a search party was formed. It was agreed that all the villages affected would combine to form a force of skilled warrior hunter-trackers. This force would put an end to the theft, chaos, destruction. The villages made their decision to leave earlier that day, the day after Serra had left. This gathering of men will bring the boys home, prisoners who will await the decision of the council.

There is a cluster of warriors from each tribe, the best they have, all with different levels of experience in hunting, tracking and containing, some new, some seasoned. All can fight if they need to. They have agreed to avoid violence till the last. They number over a hundred. It is believed there are up to a hundred Lost Boys, no one knows for sure. Lorkan is among the men from the River Tribe. He is fast of foot and one of the best hunters in the village.

Lorkan runs with the search party through the dark of the wide, deep forest leading north. Two warriors have been lost so far. One snapped his Achilles tendon, the second was unable to keep up the pace. The remaining warriors run in step, silently through the deep undergrowth, intuitively staying out of the way of trees and boul ders, no footfall landing on twig or branch. Each knows that the Lost Boys have small raiding and scouting parties in these woods and any sound will alert them. The Lost Boys may not be as good at combat as the warriors hunting them now, but they are skilled scouts and raiders; able to vanish into the woods in a moment.

Lorkan stays as far back as he can without drawing attention to himself. He runs easily, not short of breath. Dim light begins to flood the forest. Lorkan feels the pace change and looks up ahead. The lead warrior holds his hand up, the search party slows.

Lorkan stops, leans forward, hands on knees, catching his breath.

No one speaks. Lorkan sits down and takes out a lump of bread and meat from his pack. Each warrior eats and drinks silently, regaining energy and strength. The older warrior sits looking out at the forest, chewing on his bread then stops, staring straight ahead. Lorkan follows his line of sight. The sun has almost filled the wood. Bright light hits the tops of the trees, working its way slowly down to the forest floor, but there are still patches of black shadow. No movement, not at first. Then Lorkan sees it. So does the older warrior. He slowly puts down his food and taps the warrior next to him, who in turn passes the signal up the line. Slowly, one by one they rise, leaving their food on the ground. They reach for their weapons and wait for the call. The lead warrior takes a step forward. He begins to walk toward the tree line ahead. The rest follow silently behind.

A bird flies up from its hiding place and is immediately followed by a small child, no more than thirteen summers, sprinting away from them. No one moves. The lead warrior looks to three of the men nearest him and gives them the signal. The sound and movement is sudden and fast. From silence the forest breaks into sound. Birds fly from trees, bush and forest floor. A deer hiding some yards ahead is startled and breaks cover. The boy sprints fast, two more Lost Boys break cover and follow him at full speed, swift and agile. The leader gives the signal for two more warriors to follow the first three, the rest watch and wait. The last two warriors disappear into the trees, all that can be heard is the breaking of twigs and branch and the multiple flights of scattering birds. There is a loud crack some way ahead, then the cry of one of the warriors. The leader gives the signal for the rest of the warriors to move forward. Lorkan hangs further back. No one seems to notice. He turns from the advancing warriors away from the action, ducking low, moving forward as fast as his feet will carry him.

The warriors advance away from him into the thick shadows of the forest. Chaos breaks out. One of the warriors catches up with two of the Lost Boys and brings them down. The older warriors have no problem holding them. They are quickly bound in leather straps and tied to trees a good distance apart. They are gagged and blindfolded. They cannot move.

Lorkan ducks down and quickly finds dense cover. He crawls into it and waits. He doesn't hear it coming until the strong hand grips his ankle. He turns to look into the eyes of the ageing warrior.

'Where you going, boy?

'Home.'

'Lost your nerve?'

'Yeah, that's it. No stomach for it.' Lorkan tries to wriggle free of his tight grip.

'But they're just boys, easy enough to deal with.' He holds his grip on Lorkan's leg. 'Been watching you, boy. Knew something weren't right. And I was right. I'm always right.'

'Let go of my leg.'

'That depends.'

'On what?'

'If you finish what you swore to finish.'

'Like I said, no stomach for it. I'm going home.'

'Why don't I believe you then?'

'Don't ask me, brother. Not my problem. Maybe that's the way you were made.'

'You're going the wrong way.'

'You going let go of me or do I have to make you?'

The ageing warrior looks at him long and hard, waiting for a reply. 'You can't lie for rat shit, brother. You ain't going home, and I think you're a long way from losing stomach for the fight... can see it in your eyes. You've that look, hunger for the blade and the ruck. And you've something else on your mind… other than the Lost Boys.'

'I'm going to help my sister.'

'You one of the ones whose kin was taken?'

Lorkan nods. The man lets go of him.

'What you have planned?'

'Help her find the ones who violated her, before our brothers get to them.'

'You think you can get there before we all do?'

'Easily.'

'Then I'll come with you.'

'What?'

'They took my daughter. They still have her. Not letting a tribal pact get in the way of me getting her back myself, doing what needs be done. You think you can get there first, we'll go together.'

'You'll slow me down. No disrespect but you're getting on a bit.'

The ageing warrior smiles at him. 'May be older than you brother, but I reckon I have more staying power. Seen more of this world than you could dream of. You can use me when you get there. Help you get to your sister and make sure you get to them before our lot do.'

Lorkan looks at him for a long moment, then gives in. 'We need to move quick. The scouts our brothers are hunting will give us time but we'll have to go at a sprint if we're to get there in good time.'

'Best get to it then, eh? Names V. Sea Tribe of the south.'

'What kind of name's that?'

'Short for Vanrah. Don't ever call me Vanrah.'

'Lorkan. River Tribe. Good to meet you, brother.' Lorkan rises from his hiding place, they shake hands, grip wrists and nod out of respect and readiness. They jog away from the search party, quiet, low. Slow at first but building, quickening, easily distancing themselves from their tribesmen; toward Jacob Hill's hut.

Chapter Forty Three

RIGHT WOUNDING

Can't sleep. Want her close to me but she's keeping me awake. Want to touch her arm, her skin.

Someone's coming. Jacob. What's he doing up this time of night?

'I have something to show you, Maklan. Come to the hut.'

Warmer in here than by the fire. Prefer to be back there with her though.

'How are your eyes?'

'Getting better.'

'You'll do fine with Serra to guide you. You'll be able to reach Heartfall well enough.'

'We're going to the Lost Boy village first.'

'I know.'

Taking out the sword. Bringing it over to me.

Feels heavy. Blade's clean. Sharp. He's finished it.

'You were not going to do any more work on it. You had done more than enough. It's yours. You'll need it.'

'You're giving me your father's sword?'

'You brought it back, it's yours now. This is the sheath and belt my father made for it.'

No one's ever given me anything like this. 'I wish… I wish he'd been like this… like you.'

'Your father?'

'You've been more of one to me these last few days than he has in a lifetime.'

'Never make the mistake of believing a father must do the things I've done for you. That isn't his place.'

'What?'

'He's done exactly what needed to be done.'

'What has he done? Apart from beat me and my family when drunk?'

'He's wounded you… in the right place.'

'You're talking in riddles again.'

'Fathers give their sons wounds to take into the world. Some understand and change, do something good with their lives, others do not… those who don't, become bringers of war and death.'

'You're saying splitting my head open with a shit shovel was a good thing… a wound I needed?'

'What he did he was born to do. You would not be here now if it wasn't for his actions.'

'Father's are meant to do what *you* do. Teach the young, look after them. Everyone knows that.'

'Fathers are meant to protect, feed, shelter, love and wound rightly, little more. No man who has the love your father has for you can keep a cool eye on the kind of training you need to become a man who can contain his rage and desire and greed and channel it for good not ill.'

'You think he loves me?'

'Your father loves you more than you know.'

'He has a twisted way of showing it.'

'I have something else for you. Juno. Come. Juno is yours.'

'I can't take him. There's no way I can take him.'

'He's a warhound and a hunter. He doesn't get what he needs here. He's old enough to travel now. He'll be good company and he'll protect you. Lucky for you he likes you. You will need all the help you can get.'

Chapter Forty Four

LEAVING THE HILL

Juno by my side, sword by my side. Feels good. Best night's sleep in months. Cool air this morning. Good time to walk. Serra still asleep. Kera watching me and Juno. How am I going to be any use to her? All I can make out is shapes. What use is this sword if I can't see who's coming at us.

She's waking up.

'Morning, Storm Chaser. How long have you been awake?'

'Not long.' *She knows I've been looking at her.*

'Have you been watching me, warrior boy?'

She's smiling. 'No. Er, did you sleep well?'

'Best night in ages. How come Juno is with you... and where'd that sword come from?'

'Jacob gave them to me... last night after you went to sleep.'

'Jacob gave you his warhound... and his sword? You must be doing something right. We're going to need both. Here he comes; he's up early.'

'Ready to leave, Maklan?'

'Almost.' *I'm going miss his voice.*

'You can return any time you like. You're always welcome.'

'Thank you... for everything.'

'You'll go a long way... even with your wound.'

'I'm not so sure.'

'Scared?'

Don't admit that in front of Serra.

'Keep your fear out front. Take it into battle. As long as you have it out front you'll have control of it. Don't let it get you unaware.'

'Are you sure about me taking Juno?'

'It's not up to me any more. He's made his decision. He hasn't left your side since last night.'

'Come, Storm Chaser, we've some land to cover today. We can eat as we run. Are you ready?'

'You remember the way?' *No chance of me getting us there.*

'Yes.'

'How far?'

'Two days. Sooner if we run.'

'Not going to be much good at running – except into things.'

'Stick close to me.'

Juno pushing his nose against my leg. 'Ready for some exercise, boy?' *Time to go. Jacob is walking up.*

'Take care Maklan. You will be safe with Serra, the sword, Juno... and your instinct.'

'I don't know what to say. Thank you. *His hand on my shoulder. Time to go.* 'Thank you, Jacob. Come Juno.'

CHAPTER FORTY FIVE

BONE GAME

Sanfar sits opposite Zed, the Bone game between them. The dried, worn-down knuckles of the once massive wolf lie in a formation of seven. Sanfar makes his move and wins for the third time in a row. He picks up the bones and rolls them again.

'Luck of the gods, that's all.' Zed looks at Sanfar long and hard. 'If it were possible to cheat I'd say you were up to your neck in lies, but it isn't, so you must have the gods.'

Sanfar shakes his head. 'Nothing but skill. No one relies on luck to win three in a row. Not even my father.' Sanfar smiles.

Zed drops a small pouch of silverine onto the table. Sanfar looks at it, wanting to snatch it up, smoke it in one go. He reaches across the table, slowly. As his fingers touch the top of the worn leather Zed reaches out and grabs his hand. 'That going to do it for you?'

'For a few days.'

'Then what?'

'I'll think of something.'

'How about I think of something for you?'

Sanfar shakes his head. 'No more violence. Done with that.'

'Bones said you were good with the blade. Quick thinker; you get the job done. I'm thinking something more ambitious. Something that could get you out of your shit-for-nothing life and get you as much silverine as you need and a place by my side.'

'Sounds too good to be true. What makes you think I can be trusted? You don't know me.'

Zed lets Sanfar's hand go. Sanfar picks up the leather pouch and sits back against the wattle-and-daub wall. Zed lights a pipe, taking his time, eyes on the formation of the bones in front of him. 'I killed the wolf those knuckles came from, when I was a boy. First kill... with my father. Took us three days to track it. Big bastard, dangerous. My father told me I had to kill it. I was twelve summers old and scared. Didn't have the strength or guts to do it. He mocked me till I cried.' Zed points to the silverine. 'He was on that. Told me if I couldn't do it, he would. He was a good hunter. He'd killed a lot of wolves in his time. He could do it with silverine and mead in him but that day he'd taken more than he could handle. Smoked three pipes of the powder before we set off. I watched him move forward on all fours, looking like he thought he knew what he was doing. But he was swaying left to right like a baby. Saw the wolf stop chewing on the bone of the deer. Saw my father continue moving forward like a fool. I wanted to call out and tell him to stop but I thought the animal would kill us both. So I watched in silence. Knew what was going to happen. My father ignored the wolf's warning signs. He'd become the prey. I shut my eyes the moment the animal made contact with him. Told myself to open them to watch it. Tried to block out the screams and the sound of crunching bone that I knew was the end of him. What I did next was not me, something else came into me. I picked up my weapon, a short spear, kept low to the ground and moved silently through the undergrowth, watching the animal feed on my father, waiting for the moment when its blood lust would blind it to what was around it. The moment came. My spear hit it in the shoulder, went in deep. It gave out a short, sharp yelp then went silent.' Zed takes another draw on the pipe, watching the smoke rise to the roof. 'I didn't do it to save my father. He was gone. I did it for me. My first blood. Lost my father but found myself... as a man. You understand? Knew I had to take what I needed from that point. My father was a lover of the Bone game. His leather pouch had been torn and the bones scattered in the attack so I took it. My father liked the powder and mead but he was a good man. He taught me everything I needed to know about hunting and everything I needed to start me off in this place. I loved him and I left him there on the moor for the rest of the animals to finish him, the birds and insects. I go back to the same spot each summer. After the first leaf fall there was nothing left but white bone. Five summers on the bones had gone. But I still go back. These wolf bones are all I have to remember him by.' Zed looks Sanfar in the eyes. Sanfar shifts uncomfortably. Neither takes their eyes off each other. 'You are the first to beat me at the game. That deserves respect... and trust.'

Sanfar picks up two of the wolf knuckles and looks at them. 'Why me?'

'You have a father?'

'Not any more.'

'Is he dead?'

'To me.'

'That's why you're here, in Heartfall?'

Sanfar opens up the pouch and taps a small heap of the dark powder into his pipe. 'Making a new life here. The old life is over. My village is no longer my village. Silverine is my new family... doesn't let me down.' He puts the pipe to his mouth. Zed picks up the beeswax candle, leans across and lights it for him. Sanfar's face reddens above the flickering flame. The drug begins to crackle in the clay bowl. Smoke rises; quick, searching breath draws it down into his lungs before it has a chance to escape out the sides of the pipe. He draws it down deep. Zed pulls the flame back, watching him closely, a barely perceptible grin on his face.

Sanfar feels equal to the man in front of him now, looks him straight in the eye. 'You say there's a place by your side?'

'Just say the word. You have strength. There's a madness in your eyes that serves you well... would serve me well.'

'How do I get that supply of silverine?'

'You go on a journey.'

'Where to?'

'North.'

'I'm not going north.'

'Your choice... your loss.'

'What happens up north?'

'I have some friends who are in a good business, getting better by the day.'

'Silverine?'

Zed shakes his head. 'Different kind of cargo.'

'Weapons?'

'Humans. Mainly women. For the nobles. Not that there's anything noble about those soulless bastards.'

Sanfar takes another drag on the pipe. 'Like I said, not going north.'

'Then we're done. You take that...' Zed nods at the silverine pouch. '... and you head off. You're a survivor. You'll find your way out of this shithole in one piece, no doubt about that, brother.'

Sanfar smokes in silence, thinking. 'If I take you up on it, I want more than by your side.'

'Go on.'

'Promote me above Bones and I'll think about it.'

Zed raises his eyebrows and smiles. 'You have some courage... that's why I like you. I'll think about it, once you've said yes to the north. You get three men to take with you and all the weapons, silverine and coin you need to get you there... and back. Doesn't get any better than that.'

'All the silverine I need?'

Zed nods

'And coin?'

Zed nods again.

'When do I go?'

'First light.'

Sanfar nods his head. Picks up the bones and shakes them. 'Now, let me show you how this has nothing to do with luck.'

CHAPTER FORTY SIX

YOU WILL NOT KILL

Keep it steady for him, away from the uneven ground, rabbit holes, gorse, rocks and stones. If he trips he could break his ankle or worse. He's doing well... really well, for a blind boy. It feels good to have him with me, and the hounds. It feels good to be running out on the moors with them. I hope this is going to work. I hope he can fight like he says he can.

He won't leave your side. Not now.

Nor I his. 'You're getting good with those other senses, Storm Chaser.'

'We going through it or round it... the wood up ahead?'

'Too much wind in the trees, the storm's passing but it can still do damage. Some trees have come down. It's too dangerous and your eyes will slow us down. It's a lot further to go round but it looks like easier ground, it'll be quicker. Are you alright?'

'Yes.'

Slow down Serra. It's getting wet, boggy. 'It's beautiful out here.'

'What is?'

'The wind shaping the trees of the wood.'

'Tell me what it looks like.'

'Have you ever been to the coast?'

'Once. My brother took me when I was six summers. We went fishing.'

'Did you catch anything?'

'We caught a lobster. Big one'

'Did you see under the water? Did you see seaweed under the water?'

'Yes. Lots of it. It gave me the shivers.'

'Well that's what they look like, the trees; like seaweed underwater, being pushed back and forth by the ocean.' *Something is wrong with Maklan. He's gone quiet.* 'Is something the matter?'

'Nothing. I'm alright. I just need to rest.'

'Why are you hiding your face from me? *Go to him.* 'Are you crying?'

'No.'

'Your face is wet with tears. Is it your brother... the memory... about the sea? I'm sorry, I shouldn't have said...'

'The Lost Boy village.'

'What about it?'

'One of the older boys from the village did it. Killed Tenmar. So I killed him.'

'What? Slow down. Why did he kill your brother?'

'Does it matter? He killed him. And I killed him for taking him from me. We were ambushed. If he could've killed us both he'd have done it in a heartbeat. I'd never killed anyone before, only animals...'

This will bring more trouble. For certain.

'Say something.'

'Would you do it again?'

'If I had to.'

'To protect me?'

'In a heartbeat.'

'Well don't. I don't want anyone to die because of me.'

'What about the ones who tied you up in the hut?'

'There is no sense or bravery in killing them. Where would the punishment be in that? Once you're dead you're dead. It will be better to keep them alive, brand them with the shame of what they did to me, then maybe they will want to do something about it... something to atone for their sins. You can come with me but you are forbidden to kill anyone in my name... do you understand?'

'What if whoever I'm fighting is trying to kill me... or you?'

'Then you'll have to find a way to stop them without taking their life. That is harder than just sticking a blade in. It takes intelligence and quick thinking. Warrior spirit. I want the three who violated me taken, hurt if need be, but alive. When we have them, I will deal with them. All you have to do is help me capture them and let me do the rest. Will you do that?'

'I'll do my best.'

'No. I need your word. Swear to me that you won't kill anyone else, no matter how hard they come at you, no matter how many.'

If he says no... I have to leave him here.

'I swear that no one will die under my hand...'

'Whatever happens.'

'Whatever happens.'

'I'll hold you to that. Ready?'

'Yes.'

'Let's go. Kera, come.'

'Come Juno, time to run.'

Chapter Forty Seven

AMBUSH

Maklan feels Juno close by his side. He runs his hand along the dog's body. 'Do you think I'm weak... for crying?'

'I'd think you were weak if you didn't. I trust you more. The more you show me who you are... the more I trust you.' Serra stands and looks upriver. 'We need to eat. We passed a still pool further up, there will be fish there. Wait here.'

Maklan listens to the soft padding of Serra's and Kera's feet as they head along the embankment. He takes his time to wash his face in the clear waters of the river. Juno drinks slowly from a small inlet, lapping up big tonguefuls of clear water. He stops and looks up. Drops of water fall from his mouth. He sniffs the air suspiciously. He lets out a low woof followed by a warning growl.

'What is it, boy? You smell some wolf on the wind?' The roar of the river blocks out all other sounds around them. A few feet into the centre of the river a whirlpool moves in a violent spiral, creating a deep hole in its centre. Maklan looks over to it and tries to see down into the blurred blackness of it. Juno lets out a low warning bark. Maklan feels the warning sense kick in as the two men close in to within a few feet. They stop. Juno turns first, letting out a low angry growl, hackles on his back up, shoulders low, ready for attack. Maklan turns and sees the outlines of two men in front of him, crouched still. Juno watches the older man holding the dagger in his hand, bow slung across his front; the younger holds a small axe. The fear starts in Maklan's balls and rises into his belly. He must act fast. He wishes Serra were here. Juno growls louder as he crouches low, ready to strike. The two men stay where they are, seeing and fearing the power of the animal in front of them. Maklan lurches to the left, trying to duck a grabbing hand. Juno leaps at the hand reaching for Maklan. The man jabs his right arm up in front of him to defend face and body. Juno lands on the sturdy warrior, muzzle and teeth first, sinking his long, sharp fangs into his leather wrist strap, biting down until the tips of his teeth break through, piercing skin. Juno's body weight swiftly follows, rolling forward, knocking him to the ground. From a crumpled heap on the earth, the warrior straightens himself out, pushes Juno up with his free hand and hurls him into the river like a rag doll. Juno yelps then lands face first in the water and begins to thrash wildly, forepaws slapping and smacking the river, trying to find land where there is none. The force of the water drags him down. He sinks, goes under and vanishes.

'JUNO!!'

The younger warrior runs at Maklan and grabs hold of him. They lock arms and fall hard to the ground. Maklan frees an arm and reaches down for his blade. He brings it up to the warrior's throat. The older warrior grabs hold of Maklan's arm, locks it behind his back, holding it to breaking point and brings his dirty blade to Maklan's throat.

'Drop it.' He calmly commands.

Maklan drops his blade. Unexpectedly the blade at his throat is drawn back.

'Now drop yours.' Serra's voice is stern and clear.

The warrior slowly stands and Serra sees the younger warrior clearly.

Serra's voice is loud, panicked and confused. 'LORKAN! WHAT IN THUNOR'S NAME ARE YOU DOING HERE?!? LET HIM GO!!'

Lorkan lets go his grip. Maklan falls back toward the river, he scrabbles, trying to grab hold of tufts of grass and earth. Serra reaches forward. 'Grab my hand!' Maklan reaches out; too late. He slips quietly into the fast-moving water and disappears, his sword pulling him down. He is dragged into the middle of the raging whirlpool. As the tips of his fingers reach the edge of the violently spinning tornado of water it rips him into its centre and he is pulled in, spiralling down deeper. He tries to swim up but the whirlpool keeps dragging him down. Lungs almost out of air, he stops fighting, drifting out of consciousness, feeling himself giving up. The cold of the river leaves him and is replaced with something else; a warmth in the blackness of this deathly place. He sees the fields surrounding his villages. The tree line leading down to the river of his homeland. Sunlight breaking over the tops of the tees. Birdsong. Jacob Hill. Serra. Juno by his side. Sanfar. The tug on his shirt is slight at first, then firmer, stronger, determined. He feels the sleek wet hair of the animal against his arm. Juno swims fiercely at the edge of the whirlpool. The powerful animal hauls him up from the black dark of the river into the light. As they break the surface Maklan sees two people in the water. One he knows is Serra, the other is one of the two men.

'MAKLAN!!' Serra shouts through mouthfuls of water. She swims forward and grabs hold of him. Juno lets go and swims for the bank. Lorkan comes forward and grabs hold of Maklan's arm and pulls him toward the shore. Maklan yanks his arm back. 'Get him away from me!!'

'Maklan, it's alright. He's my brother... Lorkan. He's my brother, I told you about him.'

Maklan is struck dumb; he lets them pull him to shore. He scrambles out, falls onto his back. Juno comes out of the river last, shaking off water and spraying everyone. He looks up at Lorkan, growling defensively. Serra walks over and strokes him. 'Calm Juno. This is my brother.'

Juno calms but keeps his distance and his eyes on Lorkan. He looks over to V standing some way up the bank, watching, not helping.

'What in Thunor's name is going on?' Serra looks at Lorkan. 'Why did you attack him? He's my friend!'

'We thought he knew who we were and was trying to get away.'

'He doesn't, couldn't know who you were... he's as good as blind!'

'You were stalking me. What did you expect me to do?' Maklan tries to squeeze some of the water out of his clothes.

Lorkan looks at Maklan. 'We thought you were one of them.'

'One of who?' Serra barks at him.

'The ones we've come to deal with.'

'He's not one of them. He's one of us. This is Maklan. He's come to help me.' Serra looks over at V, pointing a finger in his direction. 'Who's that?'

He's come to help us.'

'We don't need any help.'

'We need all the help we can get.'

———

Maklan and Serra sit next each other, close to the fire. On the other side of the flames sit Lorkan and V. Kera and Juno sit close to their masters. There is silence between them all as they eat the cooked river trout.

Serra looks over to V. 'Why do you keep looking at me? I don't much like it.'

'You remind me of someone.'

'Who?'

'My daughter. They took her three nights ago.'

'The Lost Boys?'

V nods, keeps his eyes on Serra a few moments more then respectfully looks down into the flames.

Lorkan throws the remaining bones of his fish in the fire. 'That was good!' He looks over to Serra. 'So, you know where it is?'

Serra licks her fingers. 'Where what is?'

'This tribe of Lost Boys.'

'Three hours run from here, maybe four.'

'If we leave now we'll get there first, do what needs to be done.' V looks over to Maklan. 'He'll slow us down.'

Serra stands. 'He runs with me... and he runs well.'

'I won't be slowing down for you or anyone. Sooner we get to this village, the sooner I get my daughter back, get home and get on with my life.'

Serra looks over to him and looks him straight in the eye. 'No one is to be killed.'

'If the opportunity arises, I'll do what I need to do.'

'We kill any of these children, we're no better than them. We'd be worse.'

V shrugs his shoulders.

Lorkan stands. 'We need to get moving.'

The others stand and ready themselves. Juno and Kera follow, staying close to their masters. Without further word the six of them move out. Serra leads the way, jogging at a steady pace. Maklan stays close behind, listening to her footfall and the familiar, welcome sound of the wind in the trees.

Chapter Forty Eight

NORTHWARD BOUND

Baylan sits slumped in the corner of the darkened hut. A thin dribble of saliva hangs from his mouth like a see-through worm, bobbing up and down like it's trying to decide whether to fall to the floor or make its way back into his mouth. Flies buzz around him. His clothes are ragged, stinking of stale, ancient sweat, smoke and something unknown and long dead in his pockets. The silverine he had scratched together is all used up. The buzz in him is long gone. A young man walks in. He watches him walk across the dimly-lit space toward him. 'Nothing left on me for you to take, so you may as well leave.'

Sanfar sits down opposite him and looks straight at him. He takes out an empty clay pipe and leather pouch and prepares a smoke. He takes a light from the candle and inhales. He completes the ritual, puts the pipe down and looks at Baylan. 'You're Maklan's father.'

Baylan sits slowly up. 'Who's asking?'

Sanfar keeps his eyes on him. 'Don't recognise me, do you?'

'Seen you somewhere before, maybe. You have a smoke spare?'

Sanfar fills the pipe with weed and a little silverine, hands it to him and brings the candle flame to its base. Baylan puts the thin pipe to his lips. Sanfar notices his hands trembling. Baylan smokes. There is silence between them. Baylan rests back against the wall and closes his eyes.

'It's Sanfar, from your village.'

Baylan opens his eyes, trying to focus. A look of recognition covers his face, then a shrug of the shoulders.

'What are you doing here?'

'Same as you.'

'I hear you're heading north in the morning.' Sanfar takes the pipe and smokes, then hands it back.

'Who would tell you something like that?'

'I'm leading the men north.'

Baylan's focus sharpens on Sanfar. 'You? Don't make me laugh. You're a child.' He smokes the rest of the pipe dry then brings his eyes back to Sanfar. 'I remember you now. You were the one always getting him to do things he didn't want to do.'

'Everything Maklan and I did we did together; never twisted his arm once.'

'It's ones like you made my life what it was in that village.'

'You always did that, tried to make it about us. That life was of your own making. That's why you're here, on your own, getting ripped off by a bunch of children who'd spit on you soon as look at you.'

'And why are you here then?'

'Same reason as you. To get away from the village.' Sanfar pauses a moment. 'There's something you could do when the job's done.'

Baylan raises his eyebrows, disinterested.

'I know you love him... Maklan. Maybe you can make good on what has passed between you?'

Baylan shakes his head.

Sanfar shrugs. 'Then you won't be coming north.'

Baylan gets up slowly and straightens his back. 'I'll be out back with the horses at daybreak.' He turns and heads out of the hut. Sanfar remains seated, looking at the now, empty space around him. He misses Maklan. He cannot be with him, not like this. If he can get Baylan back to him, that would be something. Exhausted, he rests his head back and closes his eyes.

Chapter Forty Nine

THINK OF HER

Not sure I can keep up this pace. But I can't stop. Legs are killing me... the sword... getting heavier by the minute.

Keep going, Maklan. Keep going. Keep the sound of her footfall in your ears. She wants you with her, you know that; think of her, that'll keep you moving. Think of her.

I'm frightened.

Of what?

What'll happen when we get there.

There are not enough of us.

Feel safer with V and Lorkan with us. They look like they can fight. V's a good man, can feel it. Doesn't say much but he's solid. He's a good father, coming for his daughter like this.

Let's get this done, get to Sanfar, get him home, get everything back to the way it was. No, better than before, much better.

Feels like we're going down, steep hill, wind's picking up, cold. Trees, I can hear trees, see the outlines. Plenty of space around, must be oak.

River coming up. A big one.

It's the one near the village, where Serra screamed. I will remember this place to my dying day, blind or not.

Slowing down. 'This is the river isn't it, the one we crossed that day?'

Can see her nodding her head. Why's she holding her hand up?

'Tell me what you can see.'

'A hand. Your hand.'

'I know you can see my hand, but how much of it?'

'More. Getting better. I think.'

'Stick close to me. If we have to, we'll fight back-to-back. It's a good way to defend ourselves and each other. Can you do that?'

'It'll be good to fight with you.'

'You know how to use that?'

She's talking about Jacob's sword... 'Good enough.'

CHAPTER FIFTY

TRIBE WARRIORS

The villagers' search party moves silently through the open moorland. The leader keeps the pace, jogging at a steady speed. His face glistens in the light of the evening sun, an expression of concentration, strength and focus. The light of the day around them is beginning to fade. Beside him jog two of his strongest, fittest warriors. All three move silently forward in sync. On the back of the tallest warrior, tied to his body with rawhide straps, is one of the Lost Boy scouts. He is their reluctant guide to the village. He pulls on the sleeve of the warrior's arm to steer him in the right direction.

Lorkan and V's disappearance was spotted soon after they made their break. It was decided to focus on getting to the village.

Serra and the others approach the edge of the wood. Twilight begins to cover the area. They move slow, cautious, low to the ground. The wood ahead has been stripped of much of its younger trees making cover hard to find. Skeletons of once strong, bright green ash and beech scatter the edges. Stumps of smaller trees show the brutal, messy, unskilled axe cuts by hands too young, too weak, to fell a tree cleanly. Serra signals back to the others to get down to the ground and wait. She moves forward on her front, crawling through the undergrowth. She scans the ramshackle settlement. There is no central hearth fire. With so much firelight she knows they will soon be spotted. She crawls back to Maklan and beckons Lorkan and V to join them. She keeps her voice so low even they find it hard to hear. 'Too much light. We'll have to wait till nightfall.'

V speaks soft and low. 'I say we get up off this mud floor and walk straight in. I could take twenty of them on my own, four of us and the hounds'll deal with 'em no problem.'

'If it were the same size as last time I was here I'd agree but it's changed. There's more of them; even if they can't fight well, their numbers will overpower us. I came here for three of them. We will get them... and your daughter and leave.' Serra looks back to the village. V follows her line of sight. 'See any women, young women? My eyes aren't so good in this half light.'

Serra speaks through gritted teeth. 'There are never any women in sight. They hold them... us, in the huts, tie us up.'

'Tied up my girl? Which hut?' V comes out of his crouching position and stands, not caring if he's seen. He takes a step forward to the open edge of the wood, dagger in hand, staring into the village.

Serra takes hold of his arm, gently. 'You can't see the huts from here.' Get down, V.' He shoots her a look, anger in his dark eyes, he looks down at his arm and her hand, softens and crouches back down.

'I know how your daughter feels.' Serra looks him in the eye. 'That's why I'm here. I've been in one of those huts. I will help you get your daughter out but you must trust me. Please, we must wait till nightfall.'

V looks her in the eye and nods.

Maklan puts his hand on her shoulder. 'What about the search party? They'll be here any time now. You said you wanted to get to them first, the ones who took you.'

'No one will attack by daylight. These animals have some sense among them. They didn't just clear the trees for wood. It's a lookout. They'll see an attack from far enough away to ready and defend themselves.'

'We should rest.' Maklan whispers. 'Get our energy back.'

Serra nods and lies down on the leaf-littered ground. Kera follows, lying close to her. The rest find their places and lie down and wait for what is to come. They fan out in a semi circle, looking out, covering all angles.

'I'll keep first watch.' Lorkan sticks his short sword in the ground and focuses his eyes on the camp. Smoke rises from the fires and the blackened doors of the ramshackle huts. The rest let themselves relax into the soft moss and bracken-covered ground. Tired eyes soon droop into a half sleep, half alert rest.

———

Maklan opens his eyes. He pushes himself up on his elbows, and looks over to the blurred outline of Serra who is awake, alert and staring out through the remaining trees, across the open plain into the village.

'What can you see?' He asks.

'Red glow of several fires, lighting up the faces of the boys sitting round them, talking quietly to each other. It looks like some are joking, some play fighting... hang on...'

'What?'

'They're fighting for real now. Little animals are tearing strips off each other. No one's doing anything to stop them. They're just watching like they're entertainment.' Serra falls quiet.

'What's happening?'

'One of them's stopped moving. The winner's getting up, brushing himself down. Now he's sitting back down by the fire and eating the bowl of whatever it was he was eating before the fight. We need to move now. Are you ready?' She whispers.

Maklan nods.

'Stay close to me. Remember, back-to-back. Never be more than a few feet from me. I do not want you dead.'

Maklan is reassured by the command. 'Back-to-back.' He puts his hand on her shoulder and squeezes it gently. She doesn't react, and she doesn't push him away.

V crawls over next to Maklan. 'You two lovebirds ready to burn this pigsty to the ground?' Lorkan crouches down next to V. Serra and Maklan nod at him. The four of them, Kera and Juno line up at the edge of the wood looking straight ahead at the darkened village, taking in the details of the huts, the spaces in between, fire pits; how to enter, where to make their first strike. Each feel the calm before the storm. Each feel their blood quicken, the adrenaline of war filling their bodies.

Serra looks down the line to Lorkan and V. She gives them the signal to move round the right side of the village, then looks to Maklan and signals that they will head to the left. She rises off the ground, a shadow, moving out of the cover of the wood, forward across the open plain, low to the ground. Maklan is close to her side, Juno and Kera keep near, noses to the ground, eyes up; tuned to the hunt. Their footfall is silent on the sodden ground, save the occasional squelch of sandal and shoe in puddles. They move forward, steady and slow. Maklan's ears alert to the tiniest sound, building pictures in his mind of what lies ahead. His vision is clearer for the constant squinting but still full of blurs, shapes, outlines of the village ahead. Confidence in him builds with each step. He touches the hilt of the sword in his trembling hand. He grips its hard edges. He remembers Jacob's words, knows he must keep this fear on the tip of it. He feels safer. Images come of his time under water, finding the sword. Serra raises her hand. All six warriors stop dead, dropping quickly, silently to the ground. The pad of leather sandals comes close. The footsteps stop. The sound of flint on flint, followed by the puffing of a pipe, smoke inhaled... stillness. Maklan can just make out the muted orange of the tobacco embers and the youth standing in the darkness. None move a muscle. The dogs remain motionless and silent. A moment's more stillness followed by the sound of leather on earth as the smoker moves back in the direction of the village.

The silent warriors wait a few minutes then continue on, slowly forward, bellies low to the ground. They reach the centre of the open plain and split, V and Lorkan to the right, Maklan, Serra and dogs to the left. As he senses the two older warriors move further from them, Maklan feels his fear rise.

Serra and Maklan crawl slowly forward, Kera and Juno by their sides, obedient, quiet, focused. Maklan smells the stench of human shit. The image of his last day in his village with his father follows, the flies, the stench, heat, the swaying motion of Baylan as he mocked him, hit him with the shovel. He nudges Serra. She turns and looks at him, trying to make out the expression on his face through the darkness. He gestures for them to move on. She nods. They work their way round the back of the shithouse, into the heart of the village.

The sound of arguing can be heard some way ahead. Serra leads the way toward a cluster of huts. The one she was held in is there. Outside one of them, a small boy stands guard with a spear too big for him. He looks bored, out of place, tired. Serra moves close to Maklan and gives him the signal that they will have to deal with him. Maklan nods and draws his dagger. Serra commands Kera to stay, Maklan repeats the command to Juno and follows Serra to the back of the hut. He goes right, she to the left. Before the boy realises what's happening Serra has covered his mouth with her hand and brought him down. Maklan lands on top of him and holds him still. No sound gets out of him. Maklan brings his mouth close to his ear, holding his blade to his neck.

'What's in this hut?'

The boy bucks his body in protest, glaring at Maklan through the darkness. 'You better tell me or this blade will go in... and stay in. I'm going to take my hand away. No warnings, to anyone. Happy to cut your tongue out if I have to.' Serra puts her hand on Maklan's shoulder to calm him, remind him of his promise. He nods, then pushes the blade into the boy's neck, forcing a dent in the skin, not breaking it. 'I'm going to take my hand away from your mouth, you raise your voice one bit, the blade goes in, understand?'

The boy looks up at Maklan then at Serra as if weighing up the seriousness of the threat then brings his eyes back to Maklan and nods once. Maklan slowly removes his hand from the boy's mouth. 'What's in this hut?'

The boy takes a minute to catch his breath. 'I don't know.'

The blade is pushed a little further into his neck, the tip threatening to pierce skin. 'I'm warning you, you little shit.'

'I swear I don't know. I came to the village at sunrise.' The false front in his eyes is gone, his voice trembling. 'They told me to keep an eye on it, don't let anyone in or out, they said. Just stand here. Said if I fell asleep I'd be beaten. They didn't tell me what's in there, told me if I looked I'd be thrown out the village. Just stand guard with this stupid spear, that's what they told me. I swear I don't know.'

Maklan glares down at his darkened face trying to figure out if he's lying. He looks up at Serra. 'Keep an eye on him. If he moves or squeals or does anything to get away...'

'Let me go in. I know what's in there. This needs to be done by a woman.'

Maklan thinks a moment then nods.

She rises and walks to the blackened doorway of the hut, takes a deep breath and steps in. She smells it first, then feels it. Fear. Heat. Sweat.

'How many of you are in here?' She whispers. There is no response at first only shuffling. She gets down on all fours and crawls into the first corner of the hut. ' It's alright. I'm here to get you out.' How many are you?' She feels forward into the black, reaching out to touch the shivering female figure. She cuts the straps holding the girl's legs and hands together. Within a few minutes three women are free.

'Who are you?' The woman's voice is broken.

'Serra, of the River Tribe. I'm going to get you out of here.'

'No. As long as I'm in here, maybe I get to stay alive. You take us out there, we get caught, they'll chuck us to the dogs.'

'Come... please. I know how you feel right now. We won't be seen.'

'How do you know?' The voice is bitter. 'You don't know what those little bastards have done to us.'

'I was here, in a hut just like this. The man outside holding the guard prisoner came and rescued me, just as I'm doing for you now. Come, we must go.'

Another voice comes from the other side of the hut. 'Do you have any spare weapons?'

'We have three blades between us, enough to protect you. Is one of you the daughter of a man called V?' No response. 'He is here, on the other side of the village.'

Serra hears weeping from the girl in the dark. V's daughter speaks through tears. 'I want to see him. Get me out of here... please.'

'Follow me. Bring your bindings.' Serra moves out of the hut. Maklan is still holding the boy guard down. 'Use your bindings to tie him up, take him in the hut and make sure he is properly gagged. He's new here and scared, there is no need to harm him.'

The three freed women bind him. One takes hold of his face, covering his mouth with her hand and drags him into the hut. The other two follow.

They come out a few moments later, crouching low, looking at Serra for the next move. There is a sudden cheer from a group of boys sitting round a fire. More shouting follows, then what sounds like another fight, then cheering, the shouting of the two names attacking each other are chanted over and over, filling the darkness around them. Serra signals to make a run for it. She leads the way, Kera close to her, Maklan right behind, followed by Juno and the three women. None say a word, all move single file, fast and silent.

They reach the shithouse hut again. All cover their noses as they head round the back to the edge of the village. Serra spots the black outlines of something on the ground. Her stomach twists in fear. 'Stop,' she whispers. 'Get down.' They follow her instructions. Serra looks ahead, waiting for the attack. None comes. She moves slowly forward, breathing short and shallow, keeping her fear in her belly. The figures on the ground, equally spaced apart, do not move. She moves closer. Still no movement. She finds the courage to speak. 'Who's there?' No response. 'Why are you waiting? If you're going to attack, do it. '

'Serra? Is that you?

'Denmar?'

'Yes.'

'What are you doing here?!'

'I'd ask you the same. You should be home in the village.'

'Who is with you?'

'Men. A lot of them. From all the villages. We are taking these boys home... tonight.'

Serra nods. 'We need to get these women out.'

Denmar nods and signals to the shadow men on his left and right. They move silently aside, creating a space for them to walk through.

'Thank you,' Serra whispers as they move beyond the shit-house. Two minutes later they're on the open plain, low to the ground. Serra comes close to them and whispers. 'Head for the broken tree line, keep walking, head down toward the sound of the river, there is a place that's easy to cross, not too deep, keep in a straight line, keep going, keep walking. Can you find your way back to your villages?'

The second woman speaks clear and strong. 'I know my way along the river. Once we get there we can find our way. What will you do now?'

'We're going back.'

'Those children may be young but they're dangerous and they don't stop. We must leave together.'

'There will be enough help. Those children did to me what they did to you. They need a lesson.' The two women look at each other in knowing silence, then make ready to part. They thank Maklan, squeezing his hand. V's daughter stands mute, staring at Serra.

'What is it? You have to go. Now!'

'I want to see my father. You said he would be here. I'm not leaving till I see him. He came for me, I want to leave with him.'

'He will come. You have to go. He needs to help us. He has to...' Serra stops mid sentence. 'Someone's coming, get down.' She pulls the girl to the ground, Maklan quickly follows suit. The other two women crouch a few yards ahead in the darkness. Heavy footsteps splat through the mud then abruptly stop a few feet from them. 'Tara? Where are you? I heard you. I know you're there. Where are you? It's alright, child, it's me, your father.'

'Father?'

'I'm here. You're safe. Come.'

Tara quickly rises from the ground, stumbling toward the famil-iar black outline of her father. Lorkan stands close, silent, waiting.

Serra wants to interrupt the reunion but holds back, watching father and daughter embrace in the darkness, listening to Tara's muffled sobs. In that moment of stillness, before battle, she misses her own father more than ever. She too wants home.

V looks down at Serra and Maklan. 'I've done what's needed. I have what I came for. There's a group of the little bastards tied up and gagged by the second hut. The other warriors are here. You will have all you need to deal with the rest of them.'

Maklan's speaks. 'We need you here V.'

'They're circling the village as I speak. I have what I came for. Now it's time to help your woman get what she came for.' V reaches out his hand, Maklan senses it, comfortable in the darkness, taking hold he shakes it. Serra walks forward and hugs V, then Tara. There are no more words. V and Tara move into the dark toward the other two women, the four of them vanish into the tree line in silence.

Serra waits until they are fully out of sight. She turns and looks at Maklan and Lorkan.

'Are you ready?'

They nod.

Lorkan steps closer. 'You and Maklan go ahead. I'll keep keep an eye behind us.'

'No one dies.' Serra waits for a response.

'Maklan and Lorkan speak in unison. 'No one dies.'

They turn and head back for the village. Serra leads. Maklan follows close, letting her be the night eyes to his now well-tuned body sense. They move forward. The sound of the fighting around the fire has died down. An unusual silence has fallen across the village. Both Maklan and Serra have the same bad feeling. Both feel they should head back to the tree line and wait, but their legs keep moving forward, toward the dead heart of the village. They keep moving. Lorkan stays behind. He doesn't hear the single, massive, boy warrior come up behind him. The impact forces him to the earth with a sickening thud. Maklan and Serra turn to the sound of their fellow warrior hitting the ground. When the spear tip jabs into Maklan's back, painful though it is, sudden and life-threatening, there is relief.

It has begun.

Serra looks at Maklan's still face. Behind him, a cluster of shadows, a black outline of three boys, standing still in the darkness, holding Maklan in place with the point of the spear, waiting for something to happen. Juno and Kera cling low to the ground, ready to attack, waiting. Serra and Maklan simultaneously command their animals to hold fast.

'Did a bad thing back there. Stupid thing. Dakar will be very unhappy when he hears about it. They were three of the best we had. They loved it... us.'

It's all Serra can do to stop herself from attacking him. One of the three steps forward, face dimly lit by the nearest fire. He leers at her. 'You look familiar. I seen you before?'

Serra does not speak.

He shrugs his shoulders. 'You'll make up for some of the loss. Never know, the three we just sent to get the other women back might mean we end up with more than we had this morning.' He grimaces at her. Foetid meat breath rolls from his mouth into her nose. She doesn't flinch. 'What you doing here, bitch?'

'Take the spear away from him.' She holds his glare.

He snorts a laugh to himself. The other two follow suit. 'Or what?'

Serra replies calmly. 'Or I'll take your eye out.'

'You... take my eye... you come here, to our village, let our women go, threaten me with an eyeballing. You have balls, woman, give you that.'

'This isn't a village. This is a place of violation.'

'Brave mouth for a woman. Wonder what else it's good for?'

Serra draws her blade, steps forward. Before the boy has time to react she brings it round the back of his legs, cutting the tendon behind his knee. He falls to the ground in too much pain to scream. Maklan turns, takes the spear out of his captor's hand, twists it round and brings it down into the boy's foot, then lurches forward, forcing his hand over the boy's mouth. Serra straddles her victim's back, quickly covering his mouth to muffle the low agonising moan rising. The third shadow boy breaks away and runs toward the centre of the camp shouting his terrified alarm. Serra looks up and sees the shadows of warriors moving toward her. She feels no threat. Denmar comes into sight. 'Looks like you have this one in hand.'

Serra nods. Denmar looks down at Maklan and his captive, smiles then move forward into the dark. The rest of the search party move silently around the outside of the village, keeping eyes on the light cast by fires. One by one they get down, crawling on their bellies like wolves, getting into position. Slowly but surely they surround the entire village.

And the Lost Boys prepare for war.

Maklan looks over to the huddled figure of Serra as she waits for her victim to slowly lose consciousness. 'He's going to bleed to death. I thought you said no death?'

'Neither of them will die.' Serra tears off two strips of cloth from her deerskin and ties them round the knee wound to stem the flow of blood. 'Juno, Kera, come.' The dogs obey. She beckons Maklan forward. 'Stay close.'

Maklan lets go of the spear stuck in the boy's foot; the boy drops to the ground whimpering like a baby, holding the shaft, dumbfounded.

'Where is Lorkan?' Maklan whispers.

'He will come. He always does.'

Serra and Maklan hide in the large, empty hut. They hear the building commotion of young men's voices coming closer, the clatter of weapons, sprinting sandals on earth.

'We don't stand a chance, even if Lorkan and all the others come. There are too many of them. We need V. Must be over a hundred of them out there. They must outnumber the other warriors?' Maklan rubs his forehead, pacing up and down in the darkness of the hut. 'We will die.'

Serra puts her hand on his shoulder. 'No one's going to die here. Not them, not us. Punishment yes, death no. There's plenty more ways to fight than spear and sword.'

'I don't get the feeling these boys have the same thinking...'

'Keep your weapon out front and your shoulder next to mine, keep contact with me, don't move away from me whatever happens.'

They fall silent. Serra looks through the crack in the deer-skin-covered door, listening to the sounds of frenzied movement outside; getting closer by the second.

Serra whispers. 'They have found the two we wounded.'

Maklan touches her arm with his, she pushes into him, each feeling their warmth, the reassurance of the other's strength; a determination to protect, whatever happens. Serra feels her feet rooted to the spot; unable to move.

'Are you alright?' Maklan's voice, tender in the darkness, jolts her out of her paralysis.

'Just scared.'

Maklan nods. 'Won't be long now. It sounds like they're circling round the hut.' He grips the hilt of his sword. 'Where is he?'

'Who?'

'Lorkan.'

'He'll be alright.'

They hear the wounded boy's voice outside the hut. 'They're in there, hiding, a woman and a boy. They have weapons. Someone get this spear out of my foot!'

The light coming through the crack in the doorway from the fires dims. Maklan and Serra hold their breath, looking straight ahead into the newly-formed darkness. The shadows in the doorway move into the hut, followed by more and more. Maklan grabs hold of Serra's hand, squeezing it to give her the signal. He draws his sword. He knows her presence like it were his own. A deep silence fills the space. Serra's words and voice are clear and sharp. 'Go for the legs, no one dies.'

Maklan moves forward in the dark, confident of dealing with the danger in front of him, comfortable, powerful in the dark. Serra stays right next to him. He takes another step forward, draws his sword and thrusts it into the flesh of the leg in front of him. The wounding is instantly followed by wailing pain. Maklan pulls the blade out, moving forward thrusting low and quick into the leg of the next boy. His systematic attack continues as he heads for the door. Further cries follow behind as Serra makes her own strikes into the legs of others coming at them. Maklan feels the cooler air as he reaches the doorway, followed by the whack of a hand on his chest, then the tip of a blade. He raises his sword. It is knocked easily out of his hand. The tip of the blade pushes into in his chest, almost breaking skin. He hears the barks and growls of Kera and Juno as they are overpowered. His heart sinks. He pushes against the hand holding him back.

'Where you going, brother?' He recognises the voice: the leader from the first night in this village. He pushes his hand against the leader's chest forcing him and his blade back. Maklan is grabbed by many hands. He hears Serra's struggle as she too is overpowered. She is brought out of the hut, held tight by two warriors. The leader walks up to Maklan. 'You came back, after what you did... and with her.'

Maklan's arms are held tight behind his back. 'I took nothing that belonged to you.'

'But you did.' The leader looks over to Serra. 'We took this one fair and square. If villagers can't look after their own... that's not our problem. You get lazy someone'll come along and take from you.'

'Exactly. Let us go, your village is surrounded by warriors far more dangerous than you.'

'Strikes me you're outnumbered.' He looks over to Serra. 'Where did the women go?'

Serra spits at his feet.

The leader takes hold of her hair and pulls her to him. 'You're going to pay for getting away, for coming back. That's a promise. You will be in my hut tonight...'

The boys around them jeer at their leader's words, rattling weapons against shield. Serra is led away. Maklan tries to push forward. He is held back.

The leader looks at him. 'So, what to do with you, Maklan of the Deer Tribe of the north?'

The unbroken, high-pitched voice of a child shouts out. 'Feed him to the boars!!' They'll clean his bones by morning, then I can wear his skinny, fingers round my neck.'

Juno and Kera are muzzled, legs tied, flipped upside down and hung from long poles of freshly-cut ash and led away. Maklan wonders why the search party has not attacked. Where has Serra been taken, the dogs.

He prays hard for help.

CHAPTER FIFTY ONE

BURDEN OF LEADERSHIP

Where have they taken Maklan?

I have to get out.

Where are the other warriors? Why haven't they attacked?

This hut is different.

It's his hut...

... the leader.

It's him. Please Thunor, don't let this happen again.

He's sitting down, lighting a pipe.

It smells like silverine.

I feel sick.

Why are you staring at me like that? 'What do you want with me?'

'I'm sorry about my men. They won't come near you again.'

'Why try to give me comfort?'

'I wasn't one of the ones who came to you when you were first here.'

'It makes no difference. You're the leader of this tribe of children so everything that happens comes back to you.'

'The burden of leadership.'

'What do you want with me?' *I need water.*

'To make an example. Make them think I'm getting my way with you, punishing you and your man for the attack. As you say... I'm the leader and leading has to be done... or I lose control and all this... falls apart.'

Why are you getting up? Walking over to me? 'I'm warning you. I'll die before I let any of you touch me again.'

Don't trust him Serra. 'Do you have any water?'

'It's diseased, even the river water. Dead stag poisoned it. Beer's all gone. Safest we have now is mead. It's from your village.'

Drink it, Serra. Whatever is going on here, he doesn't want you drugged, or dead.

Not yet.

Lorkan will be here soon. And the others. Maklan?

CHAPTER FIFTY TWO

BROKEN AGREEMENT

It's over.

Back-to-back, that's what you agreed and here you are, back in this rat-infested village, a prisoner. What you going to do now, Maklan?

Keep going.

Get out.

Escape.

Roll over... to the door.

Two of them blocking it.

'What's our leader going to do with the woman?'

'Same as everyone else.'

'Wouldn't mind a go myself.'

Must get to her. Have to get out. Even if I have to kill one of them, both of them.

You made an agreement.

I'll never forgive myself if it happens to her again.

She won't forgive you if you break your word. Use your head to get out of here, not weapons.

Use your head.

And your heart.

CHAPTER FIFTY THREE

JUNO

Juno hangs upside down, legs tied to the ash pole, looking up at the stars then round at the camp, fires, huts, Kera hanging next to him. She doesn't move. Juno brings his head up and his muzzle to the rope tied tight to his front legs. He bares his teeth and stretches himself forward, the tips of his young, sharp teeth just out of reach of the knot holding him to the pole. He snaps forward, trying to get his teeth into the rope. On the fourth go, the longest canine snags on the rope, catches it. He bites down, pulls the knot toward him, brings his lower jaw up and begins to chew on the thick hemp rope.

He finally breaks through the first knots holding front paws and legs together. Kera is awake and alert and watching Juno's every move. The boy warriors nearest to them have their backs to the warhounds, facing the blazing warmth of the biggest fire in the village, weapons out, ready, looking beyond the flames into the darkness at the edge of the village. The crackle and spark of the wood covers the sounds coming from Juno. He chews through the final knot and lets himself fall to the ground with a soft thud. He stays still looking up at the boy warriors. Juno trots silently over to Kera and begins to bite through the rope holding her legs to the pole. She is soon free. Juno sniffs at the air for Maklan's scent. He moves into the darkness taking the long way round the back of the huts to where his new master lies imprisoned.

———

The gathering of older warriors surrounding the village, lie on their bellies, eyes on the prize, wait for the signal.

———

Serra looks straight at the Lost Boy leader. 'If you're not going to do anything to me, when are you going to let me go?'

'Let them think I'm doing my worst to you.'

'I don't understand.'

'Violating women is not who I am. I have a woman back in my village. When this is all over I will go back to her.' He looks down at the floor. 'If she will have me back.'

'If that's not who you are, why did you let them do what they did to me?'

'There are plenty who would take my place in a heartbeat. If they had the courage. If I don't permit them some of the darkness they crave, they will challenge me, maybe even kill me.'

'I still don't understand.'

'Back in my village, older men beat me for sport. I ate what the dogs left. My father threw me out of the hut when I was ten summers old.'

'You must have deserved it.'

'My mother died before the end of my first summer. My father beat me day and night for crying for food and warmth.

There was something rotten in my village. Felt it before I knew what it was. Left as soon as I was old enough to hunt. Found this place two summers' back. They had no leader. Just a mess of huts and fighting children. I understood them. They were happy to let me lead without a fight.'

'Stealing women and food is not leading. All you are doing is doing what was done to you.'

'This is my home now. This is where we will stay and we'll fight to keep it.'

'You'll have that chance soon enough. Warriors from those villages are here.'

'Why did you come?'

'To find the ones who violated me. Make sure they don't do it again... to anyone.'

He looks at her with piercing eyes. 'How about I give you what you want?'

'What do you mean?'

'I give you the ones who violated you and you take them to your village and do what you need to do with them.'

'You just said you give them what they want and you keep your place as village leader.'

'I know the ones who did it. Two of them want to lead this village. They have a following. I can't risk splitting the village in two. I'm prepared to let the village know I've found out about their plans, let you take them. Let it be seen as a lesson to anyone who would try and take my place.'

'You would do that for me?'

'For both of us.'

CHAPTER FIFTY FOUR

KERA

Juno and Kera make it to the back of the hut. Juno sniffs at the edges and moves forward pushing his nose into the dry grass and willow until he finds a weak, rotten spot. He nudges it aside, continuing to push his shoulders and upper body in until he is half in, half out of the darkened space. He looks around, continuing to sniff the air. The boy guards are gone, drawn by the call of the fight they know is coming. Juno smells Maklan hidden in the blacker shadows of the already pitch-black corner. The animal gives out a low, hardly audible woof. Maklan knows instantly who it is. Without a sound the hound pushes himself through the weak hut wall. Kera follows. Juno trots over to Maklan and licks his face then sets to work, chewing on Maklan's bindings. He has him free in seconds. Maklan picks up his sword, and follows Juno out of the tight, raggedy hole at the back of the hut. As he enters the cold air he hears the fearful, agitated murmurs of the Lost Boys, standing close to the fire waiting for something to happen. Maklan makes for the direction of the leader's hut. Juno and Kera follow. He moves through the darkness at speed, sensing his way round the black hulk of huts and ditches. Fear of running into something builds in his gut. He hears the rapid pad of feet behind. Juno and Kera keep close, unfazed, like they know who is chasing them. Maklan breaks into a sprint. He keeps to the shadow side of the village away from firelight, moving in a wide arc, looking ahead, using feet on ground and gut, to guide him round the large black outlines of the huts ahead. His strides become wider, longer. He lets his instincts run him. He moves faster. He trips on a rope holding a hut up, stumbles and falls. Juno and Kera stop. Maklan lies, waiting for the worst. He feels the heavy hand on his shoulder first then the jolt as he's lifted up onto his feet. He turns and tries to make out the fuzzy face of the man standing in front of him.

'Where you been, brother?' Lorkan is out of breath. 'You move fast for a blind boy. Where's Serra?'

'Where were you when we were getting attacked!?'

'Getting attacked. The search party is about to do the same. They have surrounded the village. Where is my sister?'

'Leader's hut... I think.'

'Can you fight?'

'Yes.'

Lorkan walks ahead. 'We move now. Where's the hut?'

'It will be the biggest.'

'Stay close. Keep the dogs close. We will need them.'

Lorkan leads Maklan and the warhounds toward the biggest hut. The Lost Boys begin to form groups, weapons out, trying to organize themselves.

———

The leader of the village stands over Serra, hand out, reaching up to him. She hesitates, holding her hand still before his. The room freezes for a long moment. As Lorkan enters, all he sees is a man poised to attack his sister. Maklan stands behind, mute, watching as Serra's blurred body leans forward and connects hands with the leader's hand. He is blinded deeper by anger. Lorkan moves forward swift and sharp, sword in hand. Following close behind the hazy outline of Lorkan, promises for preserving life forgotten, Maklan moves forward, sword and dagger held tight. Kera barks and rushes ahead of the two warriors bearing down on the leader.

Serra calls for them to stop. There is confusion. Kera leaps into the air, crashing, teeth and jaws onto the leader's arm. He brings her body up into the air then slams her down on the ground. The snap of her spine is heard by all. Serra cries out for her animal who lies on the hut floor, panting, shuffling into the final moments of breath and life as she moves quickly to the death place. Serra kneels down close to her, eyes blinded with tears.

Lorkan moves quickly toward the leader, blade point straight, Maklan right behind him. Serra breaks from her tears and screams at both of them to stop. The leader grabs his war spear. Juno lands on him full force. The spear pierces his shoulder. Maklan shouts out after him.

Serra screams, 'STOP. He is going to help us!'

The rushing in of a group of Lost Boys enter the hut, weapons at hand. Maklan and Lorkan turn to face them. No movement save the rise and fall of breath. Maklan looks at Lorkan bemused. Lorkan looks behind him. The leader holds his hand above his head. He steps forward, holding the blood-tipped spear in his hand. 'Touch none of them.'

A tall skinny warrior points his blade at Maklan. 'We should kill them all now.'

'They thought I was attacking their woman. They came for her.'

'We should gut them for that!'

The leader puts down the spear. 'Lower your weapons.'

There is resistance, swearing, shuffling. They hold their weapons out firm.

'I said, lower them!!' One by one the young warriors lower their weapons. The leader looks to Maklan and Lorkan. 'And you. Drop your weapons.'

Maklan and Lorkan hold for a moment, then simultaneously drop their weapons. Serra picks Kera up, tears in her eyes. She moves to the back of the hut, putting Kera in her lap, stroking her still-warm face.

The leader sits down heavily on his bed. 'We have another problem brothers, more serious than this.' The young warriors look at him expectantly. 'There are a few among us who would want to wreck what we have. Break it up with their need to take my place as your leader, lead our village in another direction... and if I know these men it won't be long before what we've built is destroyed and we're forced back to our old villages. None of us want that.'

The warriors nod in agreement.

'Anfar, Rednan and Sorfar. I've had them watched. They have made plans to take over. They violated this woman. This is why she came. I say we let them take them and be done with them. Let their villages deal with them. We have enough to deal with.'

There is a new kind of silence in the hut. Maklan and Lorkan stand rigid, unmoving. Maklan hears it first, ears more tuned than the rest. The sound of commotion coming from outside the camp, on the edges, near the open plain, then a far-off shout. The leader looks beyond the men standing in front of him to his doorway. One by one the rest of the young men hear it. The sound outside becomes louder. The rapid panic running of many feet, the roar of deep warrior song coming from the edges of the village. The sound of many shouting instructions to each other, the clattering of weapons, the barking of wardogs.

The leader stands. 'We will have to wait for the judgement to fall on the traitor brothers. We are being attacked.'

———

The search party is standing, encircling the Lost Boy village. Each man holds a flaming torch in one hand and a club in the other. There is no more than ten feet between each of them. No Lost Boy will get through the line. They run at the lines of warriors, screaming, chaotic weapon-wielding animals. None make contact with the imposing, silent tribe-warriors. Each avoids the oncoming blade with ease, taking the legs of the young warriors out from under them with heavy sticks. All the young warriors see of their attackers are the half-lit shadows of tall, powerful men they think they recognise from their own villages; fathers, brothers, uncles, elders. Silent faces lit by the fires of the village. Strands of ivy vine are tied round arms and legs, the boys gathered in clusters of ten, tied together so tight they can barely move, only their wounded legs free to walk home. The sound of fighting begins to fade.

The search party leads the last of the Lost Boys from the place they had thought was home. The village is torched, hut-to-hut. The boys are led, ivy bound, in silence up into the surrounding hills. As they reach the top, each group is made to stop and look back at the giant amber glow of the village they had created out of hate. They stand in silence and watch as the village is destroyed by fire.

———

Serra, Maklan, and Lorkan head to the leader of the search party organising the groups of captive boys. Juno struggles a little way behind, licking his wound. Kera's lifeless body hangs across Serra's shoulders. Lorkan rests his hands on her arm.

' No sense in getting into an argument with him. Keep calm sister.'

'That all depends on how he takes the request.' Serra leads the way. She begins speaking as she approaches the busy leader. 'We want Anfar, Rednan and Sorfar in a separate group. We'll take them, guard them, make sure they get home.'

The leader is distracted, counting the captives, ordering them into their angry clusters. They are slowly identified by the men of their villages and forced into tribe groups. Tribesmen from Lorkan and Serra's village bind their young rebels tight. The leader speaks to Serra as he watches the older warriors organize their children and young men into order. 'I'm not breaking them up. We need ten guards to each group of prisoners. We don't have men to spare.'

'We're not part of your search party. There are three of us, and three of them, it's one-to-one, it won't reduce the number of your warriors, it'll free some up.'

The leader stops what he's doing and looks at her. 'Why do you want these ones?'

'They took me from my village, held me down there where the flames are; for three days and nights. This man freed me and this is my brother. We can take them. I want to make sure they get back safely.'

'How do I know you won't just cut their throats and leave them in a ditch for the wolves?'

'Because that would be easy. I want them to know what they have done... I want their punishment to last. I want to be part of that. That's why I came.'

The leader is surprised by her words. He looks at her then whistles to one of his men. 'Point them out to this man and take them. If anything happens to them you will have me and the village elders to answer to.'

Serra nods. 'Thank you.'

'I'm sorry your dog is dead.'

Serra nods once more. They head into the chaotic clusters of young men shuffling in the half-dark.

Anfar, Rednan and Sorfar are easy to find, huddled together away from the others. Serra singles them out. The warrior separates them, keeping them bound. Maklan and Lorkan take charge of them. Juno growls, baring his teeth. He looks up at Maklan, waiting for a command. 'Easy, boy. Easy.' Maklan strokes him. Juno nuzzles into his legs, looking up, whining gently.

Serra looks at the three of them long and hard. 'You will come back to my village first. The elders will decide what to do with you. You give us any trouble and we will hurt you, that's a promise. Not enough to stop you walking but we will hurt you. Understand?'

The three of them look at her unflinching, unresponsive.

She repeats, 'Do you understand?'

One by one they reluctantly nod.

Serra turns and leads the way into the dark, back toward her village. Juno follows behind, close to his dead friend, sniffing at her, whining.

Chapter Fifty Five

RETURN TO THE RIVER

Anfar tries to anger Maklan. 'This one blind? Keeps tripping up.'

'Talk to me if you have a question about me.' Maklan snaps back. 'Insult me again and you'll hit the ground so hard your teeth will stay in the earth.' Maklan follows Lorkan's lead closely. He wishes he were closer to Serra. Juno stays close to his side, still limping, nudging him away from rocks, boulders and trees.

'Well?' Anfar repeats.

'What?'

'Are you blind?'

'I was attacked.'

'By what, a squirrel?' The three Lost Boys laugh.

'Enough.' Serra cuts in. 'Keep your mouths shut and your legs moving.'

Sorfar does little to hide the grin in his tone. 'You always did have a mouth on you, eh girl.'

'Ignore him, sister.' Lorkan shoves him violently forward into Anfar. Rednan remains silent, walking easily through the dawn light rising around them, unfazed by the bindings holding him tight and close to his two captive brothers.

Serra feels the dampness of morning dew on her face and neck. She wishes she were home around a village fire.

Anfar looks at Kera's stiff body. 'You going to bury that thing? Weird carrying it all this way.'

'I'll burn her back at my village.'

'It'll stink by then. I'm not walking downwind of that.'

'Kera's decaying body is the least of your worries.'

'Why you taking us back to your village?' Sorfar cuts in. 'Punishment should be delivered by our own.'

Serra keeps walking, not looking back. 'You don't get to choose who punishes you. You're coming back to my village and that's the end of it. Keep moving.'

Sorfar kicks a rock out of his way, dragging his feet, trying to slow them down. 'If they can't protect you being taken, how they going to decide what to do to us?'

Maklan does little to conceal his contempt and anger. 'You don't get to ask those kind of questions. Not after what you did.'

'That right? Treat us like animals will you then? Make you no better than us. All brothers together, eh? And a few fine-looking sisters.' More laughter.

'We'll make human beings out of you yet.' Maklan looks ahead at the muted beginnings of the new dawn in front of his healing eyes.

They walk in silence into the morning and its rising heat. Serra leads them down a steep hill toward a valley and the sound of a big river, untroubled by the increasing heaviness of Kera's body.

Maklan heads up front to Serra, using the shadow outlines of the Lost Boys to guide him. 'Where we headed? Your village is along this ridge. Why are we going to the river?'

'You'll find out.'

They arrive at the wide, swollen river a short while later.

'This is the same river... the one we came to that day.' Maklan leans down by the bank, covers his face in cool water and drinks. Lorkan forces the three captives to the ground close to the riverbank. 'Drink.'

'Untie us first. We can't all drink at once.'

'Figure it out. I'm not untying you.'

Serra lays Kera gently down on the ground. 'Untie them.'

Lorkan looks up at her. 'If they run we're likely to lose them.'

'One at a time. Sorfar first, let him drink.'

Lorkan shrugs his shoulders and unties the ivy binding on Sorfar's arms that hold him to Rednan. Sorfar drops to his knees and drinks. Serra jumps into the river in front of him. He stops drinking and looks up. She covers her face with water.

He grins at her. 'You'll never wash me out of you and you know it. You'll always be the dirty, hungry bitch from the hut to me.' He looks at her with contempt and lust, then brings his focus back to his drinking. Rednan and Anfar watch him closely. As he brings another handful of water up to his blackened mouth, Serra wades forward, takes him by the hair and hauls him with ease into the fast-moving river. She pushes his upper body and head under and holds him there. His arms and legs thrash wildly in the water. Maklan jumps up, blade out. 'What's happening!? Serra? Lorkan? They making a break for it?' Juno rises, letting out a low bark. Lorkan steps forward and puts his hand on Maklan's shoulder. 'Serra has everything under control.'

'What do you mean under control?'

'This is her time, bother.'

'Serra, you said no blood.' Maklan shouts.

'I said no killing.' She continues to hold Sorfar's head under. 'This boy needs cleansing.'

'You can't do this!' Anfar shouts down at her. 'Punishment is not for you to give!'

Serra feels the matted hair of the young man in her hand, his writhing body. Her strength easily outmatches his. The air disappearing from his lungs makes him rapidly weak.

He manages to break the surface, gasping, spluttering. 'Stop... stop... please.'

'I begged you to stop a hundred times.' She shoves him out of the water and onto the bank. 'But you didn't, did you?' She walks over to Rednan and Anfar, ivy still binding them, and drags them both into the water with ease. Before Anfar or Rednan have time to put up a fight they are beneath the water. She holds them long enough to feel death coming, then pulls them up.

She cuts their bindings and hauls them one by one to the riverbank, choking on spit and water. Without looking back, she walks away from the three of them, into the thick mass of new ash trees at the edge of the ancient forest. Maklan watches the soft blur of her outline blend and vanish into the tree. He turns to face Lorkan. 'What do we do now?'

'We wait.'

Chapter Fifty Six

FIRE THIEF

Rednan, Sorfar and Anfar sit huddled by the river, shivering, silent, sullen, looking down at the ground, anger and fear shimmering off sodden bodies. Lorkan and Maklan tie them back up then sit beside a small fire some way off, talking quietly to each other. Juno lies close to Maklan's side, asleep. A freshly caught salmon sizzles on the end of the stick Lorkan slowly turns. Maklan hears the rustle of ash leaves as Serra re-emerges from the wood. She walks over to them. They look up, waiting for her to speak.

'I want you to leave me alone with them.'

'What are you going to do to them now?' Maklan asks.

'Make sure there are no more women like me. That they never touch a woman with disrespect again.'

'Don't you think they've had enough?' Maklan moves closer to the fire. Lorkan remains silent.

'Of the river, maybe.'

Maklan tries to focus on the flames but quickly gives in to the orange blur of fire in front of him. 'It's not safe with them on your own. There's three of them.'

'Nothing will happen to me.'

Lorkan turns the fish on the flames and rises. 'We'll be back before it blackens.' He helps Maklan to his feet. Juno limps quietly behind. Serra looks at Maklan, wishing his eyes would heal quicker. She heads for the riverbank. Maklan and Lorkan walk away from the river toward the hill and the high grass.

Serra walks over to the three shivering figures huddled by the bank. Sorfar flinches back as she approaches. Anfar and Rednan fix dark eyes on her every move. There is no fear in Serra's body, only certainty of what she has to do. She comes to a stop a few feet from them, standing over them, looking down at each in turn. They do not move. She takes out her blade and holds it steady, pointing at them. The wind moves loud and clear through the surrounding trees.

'This isn't a conversation. You will listen to what I have to say and you will put it to memory. If you forget or ignore my words and carry on as you were, I will make sure my entire village comes for you.' The three boys listen, eyes down, fists clenched. 'I understand why you did it. I understand it, I forgive it, but I will never forget it. You must know the shame of it and heal it. None of you had the kind of father each of you needed and deserved. You had young fires in you that needed nurturing with love not fanned into out of control forest fires. So you took my fire from me.' She looks down at Rednan. 'You let me believe you had feeling for me. All you had was skill in deceit over a girl too naive to see beyond your lies and a handsome face. It would've been easier to bear if you had simply come to my hut and taken me in the night.' Rednan holds her gaze as long as he can then drops his head to his chest. 'The way you look to the ground tells me you know that what you did was wrong. I forgive your ignorance, Rednan.' Serra looks at each of them in turn. 'You will all carry that knowing for the rest of your lives.' None of them speak. Serra walks over to them, blade out front. They flinch back. One by one, she cuts their bindings. 'We will not tie you up again. If any of you run we will come after you and we will catch you. Go sit by the fire... dry yourselves. There's fish to eat.' She walks away from them without fear of attack, without turning back.

Maklan, Lorkan and Juno see her walk from the boys and head down from the hill.

The three boys rise slowly in silence and head for the warmth of the fire and the almost blackened, fresh, river fish.

CHAPTER FIFTY SEVEN

PUNISHMENT

The seven living travellers enter the lands of Serra's tribe in silence. Kera is is strapped to Serra's back with a single strip of ivy vine. The heat of the sun hastens her decay and smell of death. Serra breathes it, the last memory of her beloved friend. Juno follows close behind as if protecting her. Maklan stays close to Juno, doing his best to ignore the smell. Anfar and Sorfar hold their hands over mouth and nose. Rednan and Lorkan walk on ignoring it. The low sweeping hills and wooded ridge fall away to open meadow. The land ahead flattens out leading to the gates of the well-kept village of the River Tribe. Smoke rises above the high wooden fence built to keep animals out and children in. Serra stops a few yards from the entrance, turns and looks back at her brother, Maklan and the three sullen boys. She turns back to face the gates, runs her fingers through her hair and leads the way into the village.

They are greeted by the village chief and a group of elders. Slowly the rest of the village approach with wide eyes and excited murmurs. Children cluster round the raggedy Lost Boys, moving warily round them, getting bolder by the second, moving closer, beginning to poke and push them. The boys' resistance is pointless. An elder woman approaches them, pointing a silent, accusing finger in their faces. 'This is them, is it?' The boys drop their heads in shame. More villagers come out of their huts in ones and twos, dogs, goats. Two ravens land by the nearest hut and croak their disapproval. The villagers circle round the boys like wolves, inspecting the faces of the ones who brought so much fear.

'They are nothing but boys!' The old woman mocks. 'Boys thinking they're big men. Well we'll see about that, won't we girls?' The old woman cackles. A group of young girls laugh at the boys, pushing, jostling them left to right. Serra stands silently watching. Rasra walks over to Serra. They look at each other for a moment then hug tight.

Serra and Rasra part. The old woman walks over to Serra and looks up at her, deep into her eyes. 'It is over, sister. You have disobeyed us, the village, but you have done what your heart told you to do. To follow that voice is good. You will have to be seen to pay for your rebellion but you have my blessing. I would've done the same.' She brings her bony hand up to Serra's face and touches her soft white skin tenderly. 'We will do the rest. They will learn or they will die alone on the cold moor.'

Serra nods, tears glistening in her bright blue eyes. Maklan walks up to her and takes her gently by the hand. He leads her into the centre of the village, toward the heat of the great fire. Serra unties Kera and lays her down away from the heat and flames of the fire. Rasra comes and sits next to her tribe-sister, close enough to reassure, far enough away to give respect. Her face winces at the smell of Kera.

The now-frightened boys are led by Lorkan to a ramshackle hut at the end of the village; the place where they hold the drunks and thieves. The shaking boys are made to stand at the blackened gateway, looking in, waiting, not knowing what will happen to them. A group of twelve young warriors emerge from behind the hut and walk toward them. Some are from the search party, others from Rednan's, Sorfar's and Anfar's villages. The three boys huddle closer together for protection. Lorkan pushes them forward.

A tribe warrior from Rednan's village speaks first. 'Rednan.'

Rednan nods timidly. 'Get on the ground.'

'What are you going to do with us?' His voice trembles.

'Get on the ground, on your back.'

He doesn't argue. He lies down in the dirt looking nervously up at the warriors now bearing down on him. Sorfar and Anfar are ordered to do the same.

Rednan's tribe warrior continues. 'Close your eyes, the three of you... do not open them until you are told.'

The three of them reluctantly close their eyes. They each begin to pray. Sorfar feels piss leak out. They each feel the hands of men slide underneath them, four warriors to each. Lorkan continues to watch. The other villagers approach and gather round. The boys feel themselves lifted into the air, their prayers for life become audible above the rising wind moving through the trees surrounding the village. They are held high and walked to the centre of the village.

'Do not open your eyes.'

The three wait for violence and pain.

The familiar voice of a tribe-brother from Anfar's village speaks to Anfar, held high above the heads of the silent warriors. 'You know why you are here, brother. You know what you have done.' Anfar nods and continues to listen, terrified. 'It is over. I know you, brother, I knew you as a child in our village. I knew of your bright fire, how you helped your mother fetch water, your father build fires, chop wood; how you helped other villagers. I knew of the good things you did because I watched you and said to myself, there is a good one, he will make a fine warrior some day, a loyal brother. Listen carefully to these words, Anfar... listen to what I say; take these words into the silence of a hill far from our village; take them, sit alone with nothing but the memory of your actions, the wind, the tall grass and the silence of the watching animals as company. Think on what you have done, what you can do to win the forgiveness of those you have brought harm to.' The warrior waits till he is certain Anfar is ready. 'Are you ready to hear what I have to say?' Anfar nods uncertainly. 'You are forgiven brother. You have suffered enough at the edges of your village, away from your tribe, away from your fire. You, Anfar of the Raven Tribe, are a good one who has strayed. You will make good your wrongs, you will come home. Your tribe wants you back... home. You will sweat hard to right these wrongs. You are needed back in your village. You will come home. We will guide you, teach you and protect you from the harm you would do again to yourself... and others.'

Anfar feels his skin tingle and prickle with disbelief. His closed eyes prick with tears. He hears the murmur of other male voices speaking to Rednan and Sorfar in much the same tone as has been spoken to him. There is kindness, firmness, gentleness. Each boy feels himself let go into the words. Tears roll from eyes onto cheeks. Tears of regret, shame, joy.

'What's happening?' Maklan asks Serra.

'They are being blessed.'

'What?'

Serra doesn't respond, only watching as the ritual slowly ends.

'Why?' Maklan continues. 'They should be put in the drunk hut for at least a moon!'

'They've been punished enough.'

'What are they doing?'

'Villagers from the search party have come. They are speaking to them.'

'And?'

'They are holding them above their heads. My father told me about tribes who do this. He is there with them, watching... now he is helping... holding one of them up. I've never seen it. It looks so strange.'

'Makes no sense.'

'It makes perfect sense.'

Serra watches it all unfold from the fireside, without movement or reaction. Stillness forms deep inside her, warmth, rising like a small flame into her chest. She squeezes Maklan's hand and turns to look into his damaged, scarred eyes. He feels her looking at him. He likes it. She runs her finger along the newly forming scars and fading scabs on his young face. Rasra smiles and quietly leaves. Serra leans forward and kisses Maklan once on the lips and once on each of his eyes. 'We need to find Sanfar. We will rest one night then leave.'

'One night? Juno isn't healed. He isn't ready.'

'He will have to stay. Ask Lorkan to take care of him. Juno trusts him.' Maklan nods in reluctant agreement.

'A good night's sleep,' Serra continues, 'plenty of my mother's fine food and we'll be ready. Our journey is not over.'

CHAPTER FIFTY EIGHT

SPIRIT TO THE WIND

It is time, Serra.

I don't want to do this.

You must. Complete her death journey. She must go to ash, and ash to wind. Her spirit will travel the high plains. This is what we do.

It's good to have Maklan here, Lorkan and Rasra... and Juno. I couldn't do this without them.

Say your prayer, Serra.

'Dear one, dear Kera... you have been a faithful, loving friend, a warrior, a guard, a travelling companion, a sister. You have been much to me. You have given so freely... even your life. I do this with all the love I have in me, with all the memories I have... of the times we shared, the journeys, adventures, dangers, joys. One day I will join your spirit on the wind and we will travel the sky and stars together.' *My legs... feel like they're going to give way.* 'I can't do this. I can't burn her.'

'You can.' Maklan steps forward. 'Let me help you.'

His hand. Taking mine. His arm round my shoulders, holding me close to his body.

You can do this.

It is time.

'Dear sister... May your spirit fly free from these flames.'

The five living spirits, four human, one animal watch as the fallen spirit of Kera is taken up by the rising fire. Sparks dance above the flames then, finally... vanish.

Chapter Fifty Nine

A FATHER'S GIFT

Want to stay here. So tired. Can't even get my body off the bed.

That's just the mead from last night. Have to find Sanfar. Longer we leave it, worse it will be.

Can't go out there again, so soon.

You won't be alone. Serra is coming with you. She wants to be with you.

She kissed you.

'Juno? Here boy.' *Good to have you so close.* 'It will be hard to part with you, boy.' *Someone's coming. Serra. That's her footfall.*

'I have something for you.'

'Morning. What do you have?'

'Father made it. He said you will need more than me to get about.'

'It's a stick?'

'A walking stick... and a fighting stick.'

'He made this for me?'

'He likes you. He said you're a good man. And I told him he was right.'

'You can tell him I like him too. Never known anyone be able to put so much mead away and stay standing and not turn into an idiot.'

'We'll eat, then leave.'

'So early?'

'It's not that early, lazy bones. Father thinks we have three days of clear weather before the summer storms come. I'm packed.'

'Are they still here?'

'They left at daybreak with the men from their villages.'

'I need to get my face in the river.'

'Do you need help?'

'I'll use my ears, Juno, and my new stick.' Maklan smiles at her.

'I'll see you when you get back.'

Time to get up, put this stick to use. 'Come Juno. Let's get wet.'

———

It's quiet out here. Feels different. The stick feels good in my hand. Someone ahead, outline looks familiar.

'Morning, Maklan.' *Lorkan.* 'How you doing, brother?'

'Been better. Head feels like it has rocks in it.'

'You drank a lot last night.'

'Tell me about it.'

'You deserve it. Where you headed?'

'The river, wake myself up.'

'Can I walk with you?'

'Sure.'

'Need some help?'

'Your father made me this stick and I have Juno.'

'I watched him make it last night. I carved your name on the side. Not that you can see it.'

'That means a lot to me.'

'Are they getting any better... your eyes?'

'Yes.'

'I think you'll get it all back. Your sight.'

'I hope so. Need to get to Jacob, get some more of his medicine.'

'When are you leaving?'

'Soon.'

'Take care of her.'

'I think she'll be taking care of me.'

'It's been good to travel with you.'

'You too. I have a favour to ask.'

'Anything.'

'Will you look after him, till we get back?'

'Juno?'

'Yes.'

'He's a fine wardog and clearly a good friend to you. It would be an honour. I'll enjoy his company.'

'I owe you much, brother.'

'You owe me nothing.' Lorkan takes out a small leather pouch and hands it to Maklan.'

What is it?' Maklan looks in the bag. 'Coin? You're giving me this?'

'You and Serra will need it. Don't refuse. I won't take it back.'

Maklan ties the bag to his belt and covers it with his deerskin. 'Thank you. I hope to see you before too long, Lorkan.'

'Maybe I will come to your village?'

'Not sure when I'm going back.'

'You'll go back. I have a feeling finding Sanfar will change all that.'

'Maybe.'

I can hear the river. 'Come, Juno, time for that swim.'

Chapter Sixty

TRIBE SISTER

Rasra sharpens her blade, focused on its new edge, comparing it to the burrs and roughness of the blunt side. Hair hangs loose over her face and sweat beads on her brow. Serra approaches.

'Morning, sister. That looks like a sharp blade you're getting there.'

Rasra stops and looks up. 'Hey. You sleep good?'

'Yes. It's so good to be home.'

'But you're leaving again.'

'You heard?'

'You know this village.' Rasra puts the blade and sharpening stone down. 'Stay. You need rest, healing and I need some time with you.'

'He needs me.'

'So get him to stay too. Let his eyes heal enough so he won't need you so much.'

'I like it.'

'What?'

'Being needed.'

'You're needed here. I need you, your family needs you. The younger sisters need warrior training... you're ready for that.'

'I'm not done. I have to do this.'

'I've missed you, Serra.'

'I've missed you too, sister.'

'Is he good enough?'

'For what?'

'For you?'

'He rescued me from that hut. That in itself is good enough.'

'I've seen the way you look at him. Is he good enough to stay with?'

'I think so... I trust him.'

'That's good enough for me... after what's happened.'

Serra smiles warmly at her. 'I need to get ready.'

'Where is he?'

'Down by the river with his hound and Lorkan.'

'Promise you'll come back soon. This place is so boring without you. Too many old people. I'm outnumbered!'

'You have my word.' Serra leans forward and embraces her. They hug long, no hurry in parting.

'I'll look after the young ones till you get back.'

Serra smiles again, stands and walks away. Rasra picks up her blade and stone and returns to her sharpening.

Chapter Sixty One

ASHES

Maklan and Serra move through the windless landscape in silence, in perfect sync with each other's footfall. Day by day, Maklan finds his way with increasing ease; his slowly-returning sight offering up a new blur of outlines clear enough to move around and avoid crashing into. Only his feet occasionally snagging on the undulating path of the unknown land they now walk cautiously through. Maklan stays close to Serra, listening to her movement, the swish and sway of her leather leg bindings. He is relieved not to feel chased or hunted any longer, increasingly at ease with his half sight; ears, nose and body tuned and connected to the land around them.

'How are the herbs doing?' Serra asks.

'Good. Don't know what they are but I can feel them working.'

'It was good to see him. He's a good man.'

'Wouldn't be here without him. I owe him more than I'm comfortable with.'

'You'll repay Jacob by simply doing the next right thing. Use his teaching as a guide, that's all the repayment he needs.'

'You're right... as usual.' Maklan smiles at her. He senses her smiling back.

'I can see it.'

'Heartfall?'

'About three miles ahead.'

They continue on in silence, Maklan's stick thudding on earth and clacking on rock as the land begins to harden and toughen underfoot.

Serra stops. 'I have something I need to do before we reach the lands of Heartfall. This place... somewhere between my lands and the next... is a good place.'

'What for?'

'To let her go.'

Maklan nods. She takes off her cloth rucksack and takes out a small leather pouch. She unties the four corners slowly, as in a ritual. She looks down at the small pile of ash taken from the funeral pyre that transformed her animal from flesh to fire to ash, making the last of her body ready for the final stage of her death journey.

Serra raises hand and ash to the sky. 'Great ones, take her... take my friend to black sky and silver stars. I'll see you again one day, sister, warrior, friend, that's a promise.'

From behind Maklan and Serra a gentle wind moves out of the stillness. The hairs on Maklan's and Serra's arms and neck stand on end. A shiver of recognition runs through them both. The ashes begin to rise slowly from the pile; the wind intensifies, lifting the last of Kera in a gently swirling cloud of grey and white. They watch as it rises high and vanishes into the darkening dusk.

Tears fill Serra's eyes. She watches until the last of her animal sister is gone. She holds her hand up until her arm begins to shake. Maklan takes her hand and pulls her gently toward him. She resists, tears falling into his hands. Neither of them notice the vanishing of the wind and the return of stillness around them.

CHAPTER SIXTY TWO

FIRE THIEVES

'Serra?'

'Yes?'

'Can I ask you something?'

'Anything. You know you can.'

Maklan falls silent, trying to put his thought into words that'll make sense. 'What is it?'

'When you were at the river that day... when you washed yourself...' Maklan falls silent again, not knowing if her anger is spent or if the question will fan it back into flame.

'Yes... of course.' Her tone is soft.

'You said something before you went into the water.'

'About you not knowing what it was like… in the hut...?'

'No... about something being stolen.'

'Yes.'

'And by the river with Anfar, Rednan and Sorfar, about them being fire thieves...'

'You heard that?' Serra's tone drops, clipped, angry. 'I told you and Lorkan to leave me with them. You came down and spied on me?'

'No. I didn't come down. You asked us to leave you alone and I respected that.'

'Then how did you know what I said?'

Maklan's voice quietens. 'I heard the words fire thief. The wind must've carried your voice.'

Serra falls silent and keeps on walking.

'What did you mean by... fire thief?'

'You know what I meant.'

'Tell me... in your words.'

'They stole something from me in that hut.'

'Tell me...'

'They took two things from me.' Rain begins to fall from the two giant, blackening clouds moving over their heads. 'Rednan tricked me into believing he cared for me, I gave him my heart on the hill near our village but it was out of a lie so... he stole it, took it from me with lies. Then they took what I should've been able to choose to give freely, to who I wanted, when I was ready. I wasn't. He took the fire I had in my heart, a fire I'd freely given to a liar a boy pretending to be a man. Then they took it from my body. Any desire or fire I had for union with another was put out in that hut.' Serra keeps walking, not wanting Maklan to see the tears in her eyes.

'I had it stolen from me too... the fire.'

Serra stops, forgetting her tears, and turns to face Maklan. 'You were violated?'

'By my father... he beat me... and my brother... regularly.'

'You never told me.'

'Did it so often I began to feel something curl up and die in me, like life inside me went out. When I heard you that day... when you called them fire thieves... something rang true in me. I didn't feel so... alone.'

'You're not.' Serra takes his hand.

'Told you we had something in common.' Maklan smiles at her. 'Think it'll come back?'

'What?'

'The fire?'

'It has. You know that.'

Maklan needs no more words. Serra kisses him on the cheek, turns and carries on walking. He walks by her side, physical blindness replaced by an inner clarity. He feels the gentle heat in his belly, the heat he felt wake in him that first morning in the hut when she emerged, broken, from the shadows into the light.

CHAPTER SIXTY THREE

BONES

Heartfall grows larger as they get closer. Maklan is struck by the size of the dark city. He is unnerved by what he can make out, the blackened outlines of its huts, its dark corners and the many creeping threads of black smoke rising from its multitude of roofs into the early night sky. 'I don't like the look of it.'

'It's a bad place. We need to get in and out as quickly as possible. Lorkan has been here and nearly lost his life.' Serra stops and looks for a safe way in. 'Do you think he's still here?'

'No idea. Could be dead for all I know.'

'We should make it there by nightfall. How are you doing?'

'Good.'

Serra leads the way and they walk on toward the dark city.

———

'I've no idea which way to go.' Serra leads Maklan through the mud-heavy streets.

'Just head for the taverns, the seedier the better.'

They walk deep into the heart of the city. Looking into the many beaten down huts. Dark places full of the shadows of men. In what feels like the centre of this black place is a tavern, more beaten down than the rest, door hanging wide, hole in the roof, no smoke coming from the chimney. Thin rain falls steady onto them.

Serra scans the place with an uneasy feeling. 'Let's go in. Get us out of this rain at least.'

'I don't have a good feeling about this.'

Serra walks in first and immediately feels the danger of the place. Dirty, worn-out faces turn to look at them both. All conversation stops. Serra rests her hand on her hip, finger tips on her blade. Maklan stays close to her side.

'You two get into a little lover's fight?'

A ripple of laughter rolls through the tavern. A skinny young man stands unsteadily and looks at them. 'Your boyfriend looks like he lost the fight.' More laughter. Serra doesn't respond. The man continues. 'Looking for something? Weapons? Cheap Mead? Silverine? It's all here.'

Serra shakes her head. 'Not something... someone.'

'Sure we can oblige... the right price though. This someone have a name?'

Maklan steps forward. 'Sanfar.'

'So the blind boy can speak.' Bones smiles smugly and walks forward. 'Come, sit down.' He points to a table with two old men sitting quietly drinking. They get up and move to the back of the tavern without protest. Serra, Maklan and the man sit. He reaches out his hand. 'Bones, pleased to meet you.' Maklan and Serra disguise their mistrust and shake his hand. 'So, if I was to know anything about this...'

'Sanfar.' Serra reminds.

'Sanfar... if I were to know anything about this friend of yours... what will I get if I help you out?'

'Depends what you're looking for.' Serra puts her blade on the table.

'Well, coin of course... always happy to receive coin in fair exchange for good-quality information.'

'Do you have it... do you know where he is?' Maklan asks, disguising his impatience and dislike of him.

'He was here, yes. Gone now but I think I know where. What do you have?'

Maklan puts three coins on the table. Bones looks down. Maklan makes out the shaking 'no' of his head. He puts down two further coins.

Bones look at him. 'Ten of those will get you what I have, no less.'

Maklan snaps back. 'Ten coins for information that could be a lie? You send us off to Thunor knows where and we don't know till we get there if you've ripped us off. Seems a lot for a high-risk deal.'

Bones shrugs his shoulders. 'Your choice. Ten's my price.'

Maklan puts three more coins down. 'That's our limit. That's twice what it's worth.'

'All depends how important he is to you.'

'Eight's the limit.' Maklan covers the coins to sweep them back into the bag. Bones stops him.

'Eight it is.' Maklan takes his hand away and gives up the coin. 'He was here for a while. Tangled up in silverine so bad I thought he'd be paying the ferryman before he paid me what he owed.' Bones pauses, calling the barkeeper over for some mead. 'We sent him up north to bring some goods back. He's been gone too long.'

Maklan leans forward. 'How long?'

'Long enough.'

'What was the name of the place?'

'Tanren. Three days' ride from here. Sent some of our men up to look for him but couldn't find him. Maybe you'll have more luck.'

Serra stands. 'That's all we need.'

'What about a drink?'

Maklan puts his bag of coin away. 'No. If you're lying we'll be back for our coin.'

Bones shrugs again.

Serra and Maklan leave the dark tavern and head out of Heartfall, to the north.

Chapter Sixty Four

ROUNDTOR

Half-a-day's walk from Heartfall, Serra and Maklan come to a small village. They approach the chief and ask for good healthy horses. It takes two hours to get him down to a fair price.

The animals are young, strong and a little more wild than Serra would like. Maklan is comfortable on the high, bare back of his new animal. Serra spends half the first day trying to control hers.

'I've been ripped off.' She pulls on the mane to try and gain some control. The horse rears up, snorts angrily and turns round in the opposite direction to the way they are headed.

'You need to make friends with him.'

'You think I don't know that?! We should take him back, get another one like yours. We haven't time for this, the weather is turning.'

'Change the way you're thinking.'

'My thoughts are all that's keeping me from whacking him with a stick.'

'That won't work and you know it. Speak to him in your mind. Be kind to him with your thoughts. It works, trust me.'

'This is stupid.'

'What do you have to lose?'

Serra shrugs, takes a deep breath and begins to talk to the animal though silent thoughts. She can't find the right words at first. 'This is stupid.'

Maklan rides on.

'Wait, where are you going?!' She looks down at the horse and tries again. Forced thoughts at first, then the words come, gentler, calmer, kinder, more genuine. The response is almost immediate. The rough, aggressive snorting begins to slow and she feels the animal relax; she in turn relaxes. Maklan looks back as he trots slowly on, smiling smugly. Serra looks at him, a reluctant smile breaking on her dirty face. She taps the left side of the horse gently with her thigh, being kind in her mind; he turns and follows Maklan without objection.

They ride through the night, stopping only briefly for rest, to feed and water the horses by rivers and streams and to eat the cheese and meat and bread they bought from the horse-seller's wife. They are in bandit country. They make sure they stick close to the trees and valleys, keeping their outlines off the horizon and themselves merged with hills and woods. It puts hours on the journey but they feel more at ease, as do the animals that carry them.

The two horsemen that follow keep well back, also using the land and trees to hide and the wind to mask their scent. Serra and Maklan both feel a sense of unease but put it down to natural fear and the unseen eyes of wolf and bear. They keep fully alert, the concentration drains them as much as the long ride through increasing wind, rain and cold.

As they move further upcountry, the weather worsens, early summer warmth is replaced by wet and cold. Snow still sits on the caps of the rising mountains. They stop at villages and huts, checking the best way through, avoiding trouble where they can.

Most of the locals they come across warn them away from going any further north but they continue on, more cautious by the mile.

They finally get to Tanren. They find nothing. One villager takes coin for information and tells them where to head next.

———

Roundtor is mired in mud the day they ride in. Rain and hail hammers down. Only those chopping firewood and the two men sitting huddled by a fire can be seen. The sound of the horses' hooves is dulled by deep, mud. Serra and Maklan ride exhausted into the centre of the village. Dusk is falling. Bright white stars flicker into life.

'Let's try the woodcutters, by the barn. They look like they could do with a rest.' Serra dismounts and goes to help Maklan. He doesn't need it. They tie their horses to a dead tree and head for the fire in the centre of the village. The woodcutters stop well before they get to within earshot.

'Evening.' Serra does her best to tidy her hair. The men nod at her. 'Is this Roundtor? '

'It is.'

'We're looking for a friend. Name of Sanfar. We were told he came here.'

The men shrug their shoulders, turn away and bring their attention back to axe on wood.

Serra continues undaunted. 'Do you mind if we warm ourselves by your fire?'

'Suit yourself.'

'Thank you.' Serra turns to Maklan. 'I'm not sure how much luck we're going to have here.' They head to the main fire in the centre of the village. Two men sit close to it, cowls shrouding faces. Maklan and Serra greet them. No response. They sit on wet logs and raise their hands to the low flames, welcoming the meagre warmth trying to fight off the cold around them.

Maklan looks at Serra, trying to read the rough outline of her body and its messages, trying to figure out when to speak. She does it for him.

'We're looking for a friend.'

The bigger of the two men throws another branch onto the fire but doesn't answer. Serra continues. 'His name is Sanfar. He came up north from Heartfall to trade.'

The smaller of the two villagers shrugs silently.

Maklan continues. 'We were told he may have come here. Have either of you seen him?'

The shrugger looks into the flames.

'We can pay for what you've seen. We have coin.'

'Your coin's no good up here.'

Maklan recognises the voice immediately. His instinct is to get up and leave. He didn't come here for this, not for him.

Baylan lifts his hood and looks at Maklan without expression. Serra looks at Maklan then at the man's gaunt face. 'Do you know this man?'

'No.'

'You do.' She insists. 'What's going on? Who is he? It's not Sanfar, he's too old.'

Baylan speaks. 'Never expected to see you this far upcountry.'

Maklan spits mock laughter. 'You never expected anything of me.'

'What happened to your eyes, son?'

'You lost the right to call me son a long time ago.'

'You look like you've been in a fight with a bear. Can you see?'

'Maklan, who is this man?' Serra asks, getting agitated.

Maklan stands. 'We should go. There must be other villagers we can ask about Sanfar.'

'Sit down.' Serra commands. 'We're not going anywhere till you tell me who this is.'

'His father.' The voice from the other shrouded man strikes another chord of recognition in Maklan. Not in anger this time but disbelief quickly followed by relief. Hardly able to believe his ears. 'Sanfar? No. Is that you?'

Sanfar looks up from the flames, stands, walks over to Maklan and hugs him. 'Good to see you, brother. What in Thunor's name you doing up here?'

'Looking for you, you fool.' Maklan looks across the flames to his father. 'What are you doing out here... with him?'

'We came together. We met in Heartfall. We had trade to make up here. The trade didn't come. Only trouble. Had our coin and weapons taken. The villagers here have been giving us food and shelter in return for protection. They've been attacked three times this season already. We were happy to oblige.'

'It's good to see you, son.' Baylan's voice is worn.

Maklan's joy at seeing his blood-brother is sapped by his father's, unwelcome voice. 'When has it ever been good to see me? Last time I looked you in the eye you cracked me over the head the with a shit shovel.'

Baylan doesn't speak. Silence falls between them. Serra breaks it. 'We have some fresh meat.' She pulls the brace of rabbit from her horse and lays them on the ground. 'We're happy to share with you both.' She takes out her knife and slits each open, gutting and skinning them with speed and ease. The three men watch in silence.

CHAPTER SIXTY FIVE

REUNION

I wish someone would say something. Wish I were alone with Sanfar. Maybe I should just leave with him and Serra now. Leave him up here on his own. I want nothing to do with him. He's never wanted anything to do with me, only to use me as a punch bag. Why should I bother?

Maybe he's changed.

Look at the state of him. Worse than when I last saw him. If I'd known he'd be here with Sanfar I'd never have come. I'd have sent Serra in to get him.

Something's different in him though.

I don't know what to do.

Thunor help me.

Meat tastes good. Good to be here with Serra. Wish she would sit closer. She does that, when others are around... keeps her distance.

Say something. Ask him. Ask him so we can get out of this Thunor-forsaken place and back down south, where it's warmer. 'You staying up here, Sanfar?'

'Any better ideas?'

'Come home, brother... I mean... come back down south at least. We don't have to go back to the village. We could go to Serra's tribe. We'd be welcome there.'

'I have business to attend to first.'

'What business?'

'Dealing with the bastards in Heartfall who'll want their coin back. I'm not spending the rest of my days looking over my shoulder.'

'I have coin.'

'How much?'

'This much.' *Give it all to him.*

'It not enough. Not nearly.'

'We could ahead across the mountains of the lakes in the west, avoid Heartfall. You don't need to go back.'

'You don't know these bastards. They'll come looking. They already sent someone up here to find us. Your father and I were coming off the silverine in Tanren. The villagers protected us, kept us hidden. Then brought us here. If they send anyone else up we won't be able to hide this time. I need to head down, face them, deal with them, take the punishment. Get it over with. I'm tired of hiding and running.'

'I'll come with you, brother.'

'I know you would. I'm not getting you involved in this. Done enough damage already.'

'I came a long way to find you. We both did. I'm not letting you go that easy.'

'I'll go to Heartfall and meet you back on our lands in a few weeks.'

You will have to let him go.

After coming all this way?

Yes.

And what about him, staring into the fire?

He's your father. Maybe now's a good time to talk to him.

And maybe not.

CHAPTER SIXTY SIX

REDEMPTION

Serra lies close to Maklan in the cold, dark hut. She looks up at the orange light from the fire outside creeping in through the cracks in the hut walls. Shards of amber, dust-filled light remind her of the first time she met Maklan that morning in that hut in the Lost Boy village. She moves her body closer to his, welcoming the warmth. He sleepily puts his arm over her, gently pulling her closer. She feels his breath on her neck. At first, she puts the cracking sound down to a log on the fire. It didn't sound right the moment she heard it but she ignores it, wanting to keep this moment with Maklan, to enjoy and fall into the warmth of being with him, the welcome rest, the comfort of the deer and boar skins beneath them, the rough woollen blankets covering them. The sound... it's not the cracking of heat on wood. It's not the other villagers, long since gone to their huts. Her guts give her a sharp jerk, a warning. This is the beginning of something bad. Trouble has come.

The first clear signal comes from the rapid movement, the thudding of one body against another. The heavy breath of fighting. The struggle to get the upper hand.

'Maklan... wake up.' No response. 'Maklan!'

'What? What is it?!'

'Something's going on. Outside. Fighting. I don't think it's villagers.'

Maklan reaches for his stick. He stands. 'Lead the way. I'm right behind you.'

They step cautious, alert, into the chilled night. The star-filled sky now blackened by dark grey clouds. It's hard to make out anything at first. Serra's eyes slowly adjust to the dark. Maklan, comfortable in the black, moves toward the sound, foot down easy on the earth. Serra sees the outline of the two almost silent, brawling figures stagger around in a tangle of arms and legs. 'By the fire. Follow me.' Blade out, crouching low, she moves toward the fight. Maklan follows. He hears his tribe brother's pain. 'It's Sanfar.' They move toward the fighting shadows, weapons ready. They get to within ten feet when Serra is struck across the back of the legs with a heavy object. She lets out a cry of pain and falls to the ground.

Maklan turns and sees the outline of her attacker and strikes out in three quick blows with his fighting stick, head, body, balls. The attacker falls to the ground, groaning. 'Serra? You alright?'

'Get to Sanfar.'

Maklan heads for the still-brawling shadows of his tribe-brother and his attacker. 'Sanfar. Say something, brother, need to know where you are.'

'Here. Watch yourself. It's Bones. He can handle himse...' Sanfar is forced to the floor. Maklan sees memory flashes of Tenmar in the wood that night. 'Not this time,' he whispers to himself, moving forward, now knowing where Sanfar is. He finds his mark and strikes the attacker a single blow to the back of the head. Nothing. He hits him again. The shadow still holds Sanfar down, fingers round his throat. Maklan can hear him choking. Maklan strikes him three more times, each time harder than the last. The attacker falls to the ground. Maklan stands, out of breath, looking down. 'You alright brother?'

'You saved my life.'

The single whack to the side of Maklan's head knocks him to the ground. He feels the warmth of blood quickly ooze out and trickle down into his eyes. Maklan turns onto his back. He hears the rough breathing of Sanfar near him. 'Get up Maklan. GET UP!' Maklan looks up into the black night above him, head spinning, seeing the rough black outline of the first attacker standing over him, swaying, holding his weapon. Maklan's visions blurs. He's back in his village, on the ground, his father standing over him, spade-in-hand, swaying to the rhythm of the alcohol in his angry, violent body. The stag towering over him once more. Antlers poised to strike. He brings his arms up to cover his face. Braces himself, tries to roll out of the way but his attacker is quickly down on his chest, weapon across neck. He begins to choke Maklan.

'Come here and deal with me first coward.' Sanfar shouts. 'Let me look in your eye before I finish you.'

Maklan was once told, as a child, at the moment of death, you see your life flash before your eyes. All of it. Everything that has passed. All the moments that have meaning. Everything that you need to take from this life to the next. He sees it now. Tenmar. His mother. Sister. Sanfar. Jacob. Juno. His village. The lands around it. Hills, moors, rivers, woods, sky. And Serra. Her face, eyes, smile, touch, smell. All this in a flicker of moments he never wants to let go of. He prays this will be quick. But he knows it in his gut. This is not his time. The crack of wood against the skull of the man on Maklan's chest is clean, quick and sharp. The attacker drops the weapon held at his neck and falls forward, his chubby face squashed against Maklan's nose. Silent. Dead. The body is lifted off him with ease. Maklan sees a shadowy outline above him. He knows this figure. He has seen it standing over him many times before, in drunken, confused, violence... in his hut at home. But the same figure now stands as protector, defender.

'Are you alright, son? His voice is soft. 'You're wounded. Come.' The strong, rough hands of his father reach down underneath Maklan and lift him up. He gets him up off the ground with ease, carrying him in his arms to the fire. Sanfar rises slowly, swaying as if drunk, trying to get his bearings, and follows them in silence. Behind him, Serra limps out of the dark toward the three men. She prays that Maklan is still alive.

CHAPTER SIXTY SEVEN

BROTHERS IN ARMS

Daylight rises over Roundtor. The sky muted, clouds full of snow falling like feathers to silent ground. Bones leans against the dead tree-stump, next to the horses, head slumped. Snow settles on him in an ever thickening layer. His captors stand over him, waiting.

'He dead?' Maklan asks.

'With any luck.' Sanfar kicks him to see if he stirs.

No movement.

Serra bends down and lifts his head up. She slaps it several times. Moans of complaint, followed spit and saliva. 'He's alive.'

Sanfar paces up and down. 'Wake him up proper and make him talk. Find out if any more of them are coming.'

Serra slaps him again. 'Wake up.' She looks over to Baylan. 'Get him some water.' He hands her his leather gourd. Serra drips water into Bones' bloodied mouth. He slowly comes round. As he opens his eyes he looks around dazed and begins to quickly shiver from the cold.

'Why did you attack us?' Her voice is soft, firm.

Bones looks around at the three men, Serra, and the silent villagers some way back watching intently. He takes his time, gesturing to her for more water. He coughs uncontrollably. A clot of red phlegm falls from his mouth into his lap.

Serra wipes the blood from his cheek. 'Why did you come?'

Bones looks at her long and hard. He gestures to Sanfar and Baylan. 'Been looking for them for ages. They owed Zed plenty of coin.'

'Who's Zed?' Serra asks.

Baylan answers. 'His boss.'

Bones continues. 'We were promised half of it if we brought it back. We followed you and you lead us to them.'

'Why didn't you tell us that at the inn?' Serra asks.

'Why would I do that?'

'Give him to me.' Sanfar demands. Give him to me. I'll head back to Heartfall with him and finish this.'

'No.' Maklan looks straight at Sanfar. 'You're coming back home with us. We didn't come all this way to let you go back to that rat-infested hole and die for nothing.'

'This will just go on. I'll go back with him, deal with this and come home. I promise you. I'll be back within a moon.'

'What about the dead one?'

'Died in a fair fight. No lawman will argue against that.'

Maklan paces up and down. He puts his hand to the plant dressing on his face, looks perplexed at his blood-reddened fingers then looks back at Sanfar. 'I'll come with you.'

'That'd be good, believe me, brother. I need to do this alone. Not risking you getting any more hurt. Look at the state of you.'

'I can manage.'

'You're half blind.'

'I can get by... my eyes are good enough.'

'Go with your woman and Baylan. Head for the lakes and the mountains, steer clear of Heartfall.

'And if you don't come back?'

'I'll be back.'

Maklan looks at Sanfar then down at Bones, who stares sullenly back up at both of them. Sanfar leans down and lifts him up by the arm.

'Let's get some food. We head back south by mid sun.'

Bones says nothing, he follows Sanfar, staggering a little, looking back at Maklan, trying to give him the dead eye. He no longer has it in him.

Serra walks up to Maklan and checks his wound. He bends down to make it easier for her.

Baylan walks back to the fire, alone.

Chapter Sixty Eight

THE END BEGINS

Sanfar, Maklan and Baylan take the body of the Heartfall attacker far from the village and bury him beyond the river. With only the shoulder bone of a bear to dig with, the ground is hard work. The grave is deep enough to hide his fat body from the village, close enough to the surface for animals to come and strip the flesh from his bones.

The three men say a brief prayer of return and head back to the village.

Sanfar puts his arm across Maklan's shoulders as they walk. 'Good to see you, brother. I'm sorry.'

'What for?'

'Leaving.'

'You're forgiven.'

'You went through a lot… to get here.'

'You don't know the half of it.'

'Tell me everything… when I get back.'

'If.'

'I'll be back.'

'We've some hunting to do... and you need to get yourself a woman!'

Sanfar cuffs him on the ear. 'If she's anything like yours, I'll die happy.'

Maklan watches Sanfar ride out of the village with Bones. Sanfar turns to look back, raising his hand in salute.

Sanfar and Bones soon disappear into the wood surrounding the village.

Serra, Maklan and Baylan leave soon after. They ride west, to the lakes and high mountains of Ferntor.

The relentless rain is replaced by widening blue skies and warm sunshine. They ride mostly in silence, stopping to hunt, drink, eat and rest. Maklan keeps his distance from Baylan, staying as close to Serra as he can. She attempts to bridge the silence between father and son but soon gives up.

As they ride through the lowlands, Maklan looks up at the ragged outlines of the distant mountains. He notices a sharpness returning.

Chapter Sixty Nine

WALK WITH ME

We'll part soon.

You'll see him again, Serra... you know that... soon enough.

I don't want to leave him.

You need to get back home.

I feel safe with him.

Tell him.

He knows.

Tell him anyway.

'The quickest way for me to get back is through the mountain valley, down there to the east. You'll need to go the other side.' *He's quiet.* 'What is it?'

'That means I'll have to spend the rest of the journey with him.'

'Is that all you're worried about?'

'You know it isn't. Come back to my village with me. My mother will like you... and my sister.'

'When are you going to tell him about Tenmar?'

'When he asks.'

'Don't you think he has a right to know?'

He doesn't answer.

'He saved your life back in Roundtor.'

Silence.

'You are bigger than that, Maklan. If he hadn't, you would be in the ground along with the other one. For that I'm glad.'

Take his hand. 'Go with him. When Sanfar returns, come to my village.'

'Try and stop me.'

'I'm proud of you. Baylan...'

'You leaving me alone with my son then?'

'You've about two days' ride back to your village. Follow this side of the mountain till you get to a series of lakes. The moors rise up from there. You'll find your way well enough from there. Here, take the rest of my food. I don't need it. I'll move faster without it.'

'Thank you for looking out for him, Serra.'

'He's been looking out for me... all the way.'

'I'll leave you two to say goodbye. Safe home, Serra.' Baylan walks on.

I need to feel his arms around me one last time. 'Use these days, Maklan. He wants to make good his wrongs, I can tell.'

'I'll...'

'Miss me? I know.'

'Are you going to be alright... alone?'

'Yes. Come to our village soon.'

Let him go.

Ride.

Don't look back.

Just keep riding.

Come, Kera.

Ride with me.

CHAPTER SEVENTY

TENMAR

Just ride up to him.

No.

You can't carry on like this. He's changed.

He'll never change.

He saved your life.

He owes me a dozen.

Carried you to the fire.

Once the drink's back in him it'll be back to beatings and other men's women.

She was right.

About what?

He wants to make good.

Ride up to him.

He's stopped. Turning to face me.

'Ride with me, Maklan.'

Ride with him.

'Please. I want to talk.'

'I'm done with talking.'

'But we've never really talked, have we?'

'No.'

'I've been doing a lot of thinking.'

Let him talk.

'Had a lot of time up there on my own.'

You've nothing to lose.

'I spoke to Sanfar. Once we'd made it through the silverine sickness. He made sense, more than I thought he would. More than I made at his age.'

Just listen.

'He speaks highly of you. A lot of respect. Loves you like a brother.'

'He is a brother.'

Tenmar.

'He told me things about you I never knew.'

'You could've asked.'

Tell him.

'I've been a useless father to you, Tenmar, your sister; a poor husband.'

You must tell him.

He'll kill me for not saying anything before.

'Being away has changed me.'

'You've said you've changed before.'

'I've a lot of work to do to make it up to you.'

'I'll believe it when I see it.'

'I'll take you hunting, we can walk the hills.'

'Father.'

'Yes?'

'There's something you need to know... something I should've told you before. I was angry.'

'What is it?'

'Tenmar.'

'He in trouble again? Thieving the mead no doubt. Takes after his father in that. What is it then? Girl with child?'

'He's... gone.'

'What do you mean gone? Where?'

'He's dead. Tenmar is dead.'

'No he isn't.'

'I'm sorry.'

'He can't be...'

'I'm sorry...'

'He's at home. Looking after your mother...'

'No... he's gone.'

Getting off his horse. Crouching down. Holding his head. Say something. Anything.

'How?'

'We were attacked. He saved my life. .'

'Where is he?'

'I buried him where we camped... where we were attacked.'

'Then we get him. We bring him home. He needs to come home.'

'It's... it's been a while since I put him in the ground.' *Tears in his eyes. In mine.*

'We go now, Maklan. We go now.'

CHAPTER SEVENTY ONE

RETURN

Maklan and Baylan ride in silence. It takes them a day to reach the place where Tenmar is buried.

Baylan dismounts and walks over to the mound. Animals have tried to get into it. Maklan follows silently behind.

'What happened?' he asks Maklan, voice broken with tears.

'We were attacked by a boy from another tribe. I couldn't see. He protected me. It was me or him.'

Silence.

'I'm sorry it wasn't me. It was my fault. I'd do anything to bring him back.' Tears streak Maklan's face. His father looks at him, eyes red with grief. 'Help me get him out of the ground.'

Maklan nods.

Father and son dig.

Tenmar's body is covered in feeding insects. Maklan covers his mouth, coughing and choking. Baylan continues to dig.

They take his body out of the ground together in continued silence, working closely together.

Baylan wraps his dead son in his blanket. He drapes the corpse of his eldest son across the back of his horse. He looks back at a wrecked distraught Maklan, who looks at him for some word of reassurance.

He's gone, son. I gave you life, saved your life…

Maklan wipes the tears from his eyes.

'Let's get him home, burn him on his own land.' Baylan takes up the horse's mane and taps the big animal gently with the side of his foot.

Maklan nods and mounts his horse clumsily.

Father and son ride back toward their own lands, horses side by side, through the woodland in silence.

———

They ride into the village together. No one objects to Baylan's return. Though they cannot see the body, they know by the look on the faces of father and son that this is one of theirs. Old and young come to help.

Maklan's mother moves through the crowd, half panicked. She looks up at Baylan. He shakes his head. She knows.

As now do the rest of the village.

Her wails of grief reach way beyond the village walls.

There will be a death song tonight.

CHAPTER SEVENTY TWO

RIVER AND LAND

Maklan stands with his family by the river. Baylan holds Tenmar's ashes in a clay pot, knuckles white with tension.

They say a prayer and stand in silence.

Baylan looks at his surviving son for a long moment, then walks over and hands him the pot. Maklan takes it from him gently. He looks at his mother and his sister, then turns to face the river. He holds the pot up high. 'River gods, take my brother, our brother, your son... home to earth and water and stars.' He gently tips the ash into the water, shaking the pot till it's empty. He breaks the vessel against a rock and throws the pieces into the deepest part of the river. He steps back and takes his place by his father's side. Baylan puts his arm across his shoulders. Maklan's mother steps in close to her husband and wraps her arms around his waist. Maklan's sister walks to the river's edge and throws a bundle of white flowers into the fast-flowing water. She turns, tears in her eyes and walks into her brother's outstretched arm.

The wind rises above them.

Rain begins to fall.

CHAPTER SEVENTY THREE

BLOOD BROTHER

Six moons passed

Maklan stands at the gateway of his village, Juno by his side, looking ahead at the leafless tree line. His sight almost fully returned. He can make out the first snow on the branches, the ground is cold beneath his feet.

Serra waits in the warmth of his hut.

His gut told him to be here at this time, at the gateway to his village.

The figure ahead emerges from the wood like a wild animal, slow, cautious, weaving his way forward with a heavy limp. Maklan remembers his vision of human into stag. This human is no vision. He is flesh and blood. A scarred face. Clothes ripped to rags. Maklan steps forward, no stick in hand, fearful for the wrecked blood brother limping toward him now. He gathers himself, quickens his pace, walking toward this broken man, thinking of the herbs he will use to help heal the wounds now coming into clearer view. Maklan runs forward to welcome Sanfar, Warrior of the Deer Tribe of the north…

… home.

End

CPSIA information can be obtained at www.ICGtesting.com
Printed in the USA
LVOW11s1701250914

405879LV00006B/864/P

9 781492 326366